Iris

A Monster MMFF Romance

Sofia Rose

Other Books by Sofia

<u>SOFIA ROSE</u>

<u>Fortune Records Omegaverse:</u>

Snapdragon

Aster

Iris

Zinnia

Fritillaria

<u>Briar Hill Omegaverse:</u>

Touched & Tamed

<u>Whimsywood Tales:</u>

A Teacup for Trouble

<u>The Zodiac Society:</u>

Patreon exclusive, 13 novellas

A Note on Omegaverse

Before you begin, I wanted to take a moment to explain the version of omegaverse you'll find in this series.

Omegaverse is a romance subgenre that originated in fanfiction spaces and has since evolved into many different interpretations across books and authors. There is no single "correct" version. What follows is *my* take on omegaverse, and the rules that apply specifically to the world of the *Fortune Records Omegaverse*.

In this universe, society is divided between humans and monsters, who have historically lived apart. Because of this separation, humans do not grow up knowing about omegaverse dynamics. Human characters are unaware of secondary genders, heats, mating bonds, and related biology until they spend meaningful time with monsters. For humans, a dormant secondary gender is only triggered through meeting a monster mate.

Secondary Genders

In addition to primary sex, characters in this world have a secondary gender: **alpha** or **omega**. Any primary gender can be alphas or omegas. There are **no betas** in this universe.

Among monsters, secondary gender can be sensed instinctively. Humans do not have this ability in the same way, though some humans may experience a faint or inconsistent awareness of a mate. Monsters, particularly shifters, have heightened senses of smell, which makes their ability to scent secondary gender and mates far stronger and more reliable.

Omegas are not publicly labeled or categorized within human society.

Scent

Both alphas and omegas have distinct, unique scents, often influenced by personality, emotional state, and individual biology. A mate's scent is instinctively recognizable and often irresistible, creating a powerful pull between bonded partners.

When an omega becomes aroused, their scent sweetens, intensifying attraction and instinctual responses in nearby alphas. Scent plays a central role in attraction, bonding, and recognition throughout this world.

Heats and Instinct

Omegas experience heats, which are biological periods marked by heightened desire, sensitivity, and instinct. These urges often begin as an intensification of emotion and attraction, and can escalate into overwhelming instinct while in heat. Choice and consent still exist, but biology plays a powerful role in shaping how these experiences feel and unfold.

Mates and Bonds

Omegaverse bonds in this world are biological and deeply rooted in instinct. An omega will only ever be bonded to one alpha, and may also bond with additional omega mates within the same bond structure.

To complete a bond, two things must occur: a verbal acceptance of the bond, and a **claiming bite** from the alpha. The bite itself is pleasurable for the omega and marks the bond as fully formed. Until both acceptance and the bite occur, the bond remains incomplete.

Anatomy and Knotting

Male alphas in this universe have knots as part of their anatomy. A knot is an expanding ring of tissue around the base of an alpha's penis that swells during orgasm. This is a biological trait associated with mating and bonding.

Pack Structure

Pack dynamics in this world consist of one alpha with one or more omegas. These dynamics are instinctual rather than societal, and individual relationships may look very different depending on the characters involved.

This note is not meant to be exhaustive, but rather to offer grounding before you begin. As with all omegaverse stories, much of how these elements function is revealed through character experience, emotion, and connection.

Thank you for reading, and I hope you enjoy this world as much as I loved writing it.

Content Warning

The following book contains content that may be triggering for some readers. There are themes of segregation. There is also mention of the passing of a family member.

Content includes: breath play, primal play, omegaverse, knotting, public masturbation, anal penetration, tentacle play, internalized misogyny, internalized heterosexuality, degradation, water play, restraints, spitting, cumflation.

If you need any more information on any of the above, you can email me at sofiaroseauthor@gmail.com

Dedication

To anyone who has ever wanted to have two boyfriends, and also for those boyfriends to be boyfriends. And if you wanted a girlfriend, too.

Chapter 1

Daisy

"You sure you've got everything you need?"

Cleo nods, her teeth chattering beneath her rosy nose. She looks so cute, all bundled up in her winter gear. The soft pinks and blues of her outfit serving some serious snow bunny vibes.

I run through a mental list of what we have packed again, but it seems that the months of planning has paid off.

Pulling the shutter of the storage unit down, I clip the flimsy padlock into place. Hopefully our things will defeat all odds and stay safe for the next six months.

"Our stuff is going to be defrosted by the time we get back," Cleo says, kicking a stray icicle on the ground.

"We don't know that," I tell her. She is probably right though, everything was likely already starting to freeze since Dad helped us drop it all off yesterday.

Putting our things into storage was to help us save money on rent while we were away. But now I'm starting to think that we'll have to buy all new stuff when we get back. Being a grown up is hard.

My fingers are painfully numb from the cold when I take out my phone to call us an Uber.

"Come on, babe." I pass Cleo's suitcase to her and we start the walk to the meeting point for the car.

Luckily, today was pretty smooth considering my dad helped us out with the bulk of our things yesterday. We left it all pretty tight with timing, handing the keys back to our apartment today. We were just here to drop off our last few items.

But today, all of our hard work was going to start to pay off. Cleo and I were finally going on tour with Flora again.

Although things were going to be very different this time around.

Since our last tour together, the shape of our world had shifted quite a bit. Flora's record label had made some major changes.

Fortune Records had built a new studio that was open to both humans and monsters. I wasn't sure how I had felt about that development at first, but I couldn't argue that the monsters were very attractive.

When Flora had first shown Cleo and I the pictures from her shoot with Sebastian, we were fawning over how good they looked.

I hadn't really *seen* any monsters before then that weren't depicted by humans to be inherently scary. Now, things were a little more normalized for us.

After Flora met her mate, Sebastian, we started spending a lot more time with monsters in general. Sebastian wasn't actually all that interesting looking once I had met some more monsters. There was a lady who worked in the label that had *snakes* growing out of her head instead of hair.

We're not just going on tour with Flora though, this is a double headline with her and Sebastian. So I'm excited to meet some more fun monsters on our journey.

Our Uber arrives, pulling me out of my thoughts. Thankfully, the driver hops out to help us get our suitcases in the trunk. I don't want to throw my back out right before tour, that would be the worst case scenario.

Cleo chats with the driver for most of our journey, just harmless small talk. I'm not really into talking with strangers, so I stay quiet enough. That is until the driver asks if we're going on vacation. I try to talk over Cleo to lie about what we're doing, but she gets there first.

"Sort of!" Cleo chirps. "We're going on tour actually, with a monster band. It's gonna be super fun."

My heart stops, my chest aching as I hold my breath. The driver gives an awkward chuckle and goes quiet. Hopefully he decides to stay quiet like that, the last thing we need is for him to dump us in the middle of nowhere.

Cleo looks concerned that he didn't reply, turning to me in confusion. Her brows furrowing over those bright blue eyes. I reach across the seat and take her hand in mine, squeezing reassuringly, and give her a gentle smile. Sometimes Cleo doesn't understand what she should and shouldn't say, but she means well.

"This is as far as I wanna go 'round here." The driver pulls to a stop on the outskirts of the area that the studio is in.

I sigh, giving a reserved nod.

We are left to handle our own suitcases now, and I take them both out, trying to hold the weight on my legs and not my back. We barely make it onto the sidewalk before the car has turned around and sped away.

Cleo's plush little lip wobbles as she pulls her suitcase along behind her.

"I'm sorry," she sniffles. "I shouldn't have said anything. He seemed so nice, and I wasn't thinking."

"It's OK, babe." I pull her to a stop, picking a piece of her light blond hair out of her face. "We're literally only a twenty minute walk away. We'll be good."

I take Cleo's tote from her and set it on her suitcase, wrapping the strap around the handle. That will help free her arms up a bit and make it easier to walk.

We're barely walking for a few minutes when a loud honking sound gives me my second heart attack of the day.

Chapter 2

Nereus

Maddox and I are finally almost at the studio. You would think having done this drive so many times now that I would be better at it. My nerves for today got the better of me though and I accidentally missed our turn on the highway.

One quick detour through a human neighborhood out of the way, we're finally back on track. I think.

Fuck. Every tour always starts out this way, the thoughts of being stuck in a tour bus with Maddox for six months being both exhilarating and terrifying.

My minotaur mate snoozes next to me, having drifted off a while ago. I don't even think he noticed our detour.

The early morning sun sets his soft white fur aglow, the reddish tones in his tawny brown patches showing themselves. His large septum ring shifts slightly with each of his little sighs as he sleeps. The sunlight softening the golden bronze of his horns.

Shit, I need to focus on the road. I'm just lucky that it's been quiet this morning. My car is filled with Maddox's scent, the pine burning my nose while the chestnuts move in to soften the hurt. Maddox's scent is bittersweet, and I was looking forward to getting to be near it all day and night now.

I'm distracted by two figures ahead, it looks like two humans bundled up in their winter clothes. That makes sense considering the direction we were coming from. But why were they walking this way?

On closer inspection, it looks to be Daisy and Cleo, Flora's dancers. What were they doing walking with their suitcases?

I press my horn once to get their attention, forgetting that in doing so I would wake up Maddox next to me. He jumps to life as I pull up next to the girls.

"Is that..?" Maddox asks in his sleepy haze.

"Yeah," I say, switching off the engine and climbing out of the car. The ground is burning cold against my tentacles, but that was just something I had to get used to at this time of year.

"Why are you walking?" I ask, but it comes out more aggressive than I mean it to. I'm just worried about them being out on their own in the early morning like this.

"Come on, we'll drive you the rest of the way." Maddox sounds much friendlier than me, as per usual. He makes his way to the trunk, easily picking up both their suitcases at the same time.

Cleo giggles at how easily Maddox picks them up, calling him a mother hen in that sweet little voice of hers. She was always saying such weird phrases like that.

Daisy takes one look at my confusion and laughs at me. "It's a human phrase," she says, patting me on the arm. Well, obviously it wasn't a monster phrase.

"The Uber only just dropped us off," Daisy continues to tell me, as Maddox helps Cleo up into the truck.

"Why this far out, though?" I ask her.

"Oh, we just wanted to stretch our legs."

Her response seems performative, and pointedly loud enough for Cleo to hear. I can't help the rogue tentacle that wraps around Daisy's ankle, holding her back as the others get in the truck.

"What really happened?" I ask softly, in what I hope is a gentle tone.

"I told you," she says. "We just wanted to stretch our legs. It was a bad call though, it's far too cold out for that."

I give her a look to say that I can see right through her. I don't like holding her back in the cold like this. Heck, my tentacles were about to crack on this freezing ground. But I needed to know what was really going on.

"OK," Daisy sighs. "Cleo accidentally let it slip to our driver that we were going on tour with monsters and then he refused to drive us any closer."

My chest boils with rage, but I try not to show it. I can see the anger in the furrow of Daisy's brow, the fire in her soft green gaze.

I reluctantly let her go, moving to the back of the truck and lifting her up into the seat. The warmth of her body seeps through her coat and warms my hands for a brief moment.

Getting back up into my seat, I see the incredulous look on Cleo's face. She pauses her chatting with Maddox, her eyes widening as I settle in.

"Wait." Cleo says. "You don't have a seat?"

I chuckle, shaking my head as I pull away and drive us the rest of the way to the studio.

Being a water monster was certainly difficult on land. There weren't very many modifications available to me to make life a little easier.

A bit of ingenuity helped though, and that resulted in having a seatless driving experience. There was a chair back, so you might not notice initially that the truck was modified. But I didn't have a seat on the base of it.

This way, I could lean back for comfort, but I could also fit all my tentacles in here. Driving itself was easy enough, my tentacles were better than any kind of *feet*.

I can't help but keep an eye on all three of them as I drive. It's surprising to me how comfortable I am with this group.

Not that I've ever had much of an opinion towards humans. Since we've started mingling with them more at the studio, I've grown to have a soft spot for some of them. Like Hyacinth, Addison's mate. She's a sweet girl and I can't imagine anyone not liking someone like that.

While I'm sure there are some unsavory humans out there, I have yet to meet one. Although, I can't help but think about the Uber driver that just abandoned Daisy and Cleo on the street in the early hours of the morning.

This particular group is fun though. Maddox and I have hung around with the girls a few times at rehearsals. Not to mention we've got a lot of friends in common, so we do see each other a good bit. Sebastian loves throwing dinner parties especially, so we tend to see them there mostly.

But being on tour for six months will be different. We won't be sharing a tour bus, but we will definitely be hanging out as a group with Flora and Sebastian a lot.

I finally pull up to the parking lot and I'm thankful that we found the girls when we did. It would have taken them at least thirty minutes to walk this far with those suitcases.

Flora and Sebastian are outside one of the buses, chatting with Dave, our tour manager.

I've barely pulled to a stop when the girls climb out of the backseat, running to Flora. Flora squeals and a lot of high pitched noises happen far too early in the morning.

Distracting myself, I get everyone's luggage out of the trunk, my arms and tentacles working in tandem to make quick work of it.

Flora mentions something about getting their things and the girls make their way to the car.

"Morning," I greet Flora, who gives me a cheerful grin. It still baffles me how well she and Sebastian get along.

Daisy and Cleo grab their things and the three of them go off to their bus to get settled in.

Sebastian joins Maddox and I, clapping us both on the back in greeting.

"I didn't realize you were picking the girls up on the way," he says.

"We weren't."

"We weren't planning on it, no." Maddox pipes in, always ready to develop on what I've said. "But we found them walking about a ten minute drive away. Totally crazy, but they said that they wanted to stretch their legs."

"What?" Sebastian visibly cringes. "It's fucking freezing out this morning. Are they crazy?"

"They had their reasons," I say, simply. I don't like what Sebastian is implying, but I understand what he thinks given the little bit of information that he has.

"Thanks for picking them up, anyway." Sebastian continues, placing a hand on my arm.

I know he means well, but I don't like that Sebastian is taking responsibility for the girls. Why is he thanking me? They're not *his* girls.

Just because they're friends with his mate, doesn't mean they're his responsibility. Sebastian isn't the only alpha around here. Daisy and Cleo could just as easily be *my* responsibility.

Sebastian and Maddox start to speak about something else, and move towards the bus. I lock up the truck, still annoyed with Sebastian. But when I go to grab our bags and see that Sebastian has both of them already, walking ahead with Maddox, I soften up a little bit.

Why was I getting so angry about this? Wasn't it good that everyone was looking out for each other? That's how a good tour group works.

If Sebastian wants to take responsibility for Daisy and Cleo, why not let him?

That thought doesn't sit right with me though.

Chapter 3

Maddox

Nereus is sulking behind Sebastian and I, his tentacles moving along slower than usual.

"What's up with him?" Sebastian asks me.

I huff, my septum ring moving with the force behind it, steam billowing out into the frigid air.

"I'm not sure," I admit. "He was fine until we picked up the girls. But he might be annoyed that they were walking carelessly in the cold. You know how protective he can get."

Sebastian shrugs, recognizing the alpha trait that he also has.

I'm glad that he's off my case about it. I don't know why everyone always expects me to know exactly how Nereus is feeling.

I also hate that an alpha's inherent protectiveness is a sound reason for them to butt their noses in where they aren't wanted. His protectiveness shouldn't be a sufficient explanation, but regardless, it is.

Nereus has almost caught up with us, but his stormy green eyes are vacant in a daze. Calling his name doesn't work, so I snap my fingers in front of his face to get his attention. It just earns me even more of a scowl, this time directed only at me. The excited rush that fills my body at that look is unwanted, but present nonetheless.

I clear my throat before speaking, afraid of what squeaky sound might come out. "We should probably get settled and unpacked before we get moving."

Nereus nods and follows me onto the bus. It's a tight fit for three monsters, but it's doable. Being this cooped up will be hard for me though, I'll definitely need to run a couple of times a day to help with that.

It's a different bus than we had last tour, and I head straight to the back of the bus, dumping my bag on a random bunk. The final door opens into a room with a giant soaking tub. Perfect. I needed to make sure that this was here before we went anywhere, and it looks more than big enough for Nereus.

When we're not actively driving, Nereus will spend the full night in the tub. He doesn't *need* to be in water to survive, but it's the only time that Nereus ever seems to relax. That, and when he's on stage.

Getting these tubs fitted usually got some interesting looks from the contractors. It's pretty unusual to see a water monster who chooses to live on land like Nereus does. But Nereus was raised on land, and it's all he knows.

"You're all set, big guy." I say to Nereus as I start to unpack my things into my bunk. It really doesn't take long, and before I know it I am sitting with the guys at the table as the bus lurches into motion.

I like the set up of this bus. There's a booth around a little table when you first walk in. That's opposite a little kitchenette, just big enough for making drinks. Further into the bus you get a giant, deep set couch facing a TV screen, before hitting the bunks, the bathroom, and the tub room. It's the usual varnished wood and chrome color scheme, but that's just the way of tour buses.

It strikes me as kind of weird that Sebastian is choosing to stay with us on our bus. Maybe Flora just wanted to stay with her friends. If I had a mate, I don't know if I would be able to stand letting them sleep away from me.

But I do understand that Flora and Sebastian might be trying to keep things professional. It's also good for camaraderie to stay with your stage team.

I have been trying over the last couple days to mentally prepare myself for being the only omega on the bus. But sitting here while Sebastian deals out the cards for a game, I'm feeling so unprepared.

This is my fifth year in a row being on tour with the guys. But I'm being a pessimist, it's usually really fun. I just wish Addison or one of our other omega friends could join us. I value having Addison around when we're in the studio, that's for sure.

Addison is happily at home, working on an album with a new artist, her mate Hyacinth working with her on it. Liliana, their other mate, is working for the same artist on the PR side of things too. Working that closely with your mate must be a lot though. I can't imagine it.

Not that I want a mate, anyway. Because that would mean that I would be stuck with an alpha, and I am not about that life.

Growing up as an omega minotaur meant that I got to see the mean side of alphas. I was bullied in school to no end, despite being bigger than most of those losers. There were other ways to harm though, with words, and I didn't feel like attaching myself for life to a potentially volatile alpha.

I look down at the cards that Sebastian passes me, it's actually a pretty good hand. Trying not to let the guys pick up on it, I let out a dramatic sigh.

Sebastian and Nereus get a bit boisterous when they put down their cards, arguing about the nuances of the game and who actually has a better hand. They look to me to place my hand, but I don't really feel like playing. I fold my winning hand, leaving them to their dispute.

Looking at them, I understand that they are enjoying themselves. I just can't find any fun in that. I might be bigger than Sebastian, but it doesn't feel like it in this moment.

A softer mate would suit me much better. My mind wanders to the girl's bus, someone like Cleo would suit me perfectly. Cheerful and eager to have fun, but also willing to let me care for her too.

Chapter 4

C^{leo}

I curl up into a ball on the giant couch, my chin resting on my knees.

Daisy and I haven't seen Flora for nearly a whole week, so we're catching up on each other's lives.

"You know what? We need wine." Flora declares, moving over to the mini fridge and pulling out a bottle of Chardonnay. She passes the bottle to me, the cold feeling much more crisp and inviting now that I am in the toasty warm bus under a blanket. Flora grabs three plastic cups and joins us back on the couch, serving us.

"Cheers," I say, holding up my cup. "To plastic cups and being back on tour!"

We all giggle at my joke. We've chatted before about how whenever we're at a party and someone hands us a plastic cup, we immediately feel like we're back on tour.

A few sips in and the wine relaxes me. I had been feeling a little on edge after the situation with the Uber. But we're on our shiny new tour bus now and we can just relax and perform.

This bus is much nicer than our last one. The furnishings are all a light wood color and soft cream fabrics. It's really nice and relaxing. Flora's golden complexion blends into the space, probably similar to mine. My white blond hair probably blends in more, if anything.

Daisy is radiant though, her bright red curls standing out in stark contrast. The rich tones put everything else to shame. Her eyes are the palest shade of green, but they still stand out against her creamy freckled skin. I could admit that my best friend was beautiful.

Flora commandeers the conversation a bit, having drank her wine a little quicker than Daisy or I. I do love seeing Flora like this, she's the best fun.

Sitting myself forward a bit, I listen to her.

"OK, so there's this big national park that's near one of our earlier stops, and I just *have* to go with Sebastian."

"Outside?" Daisy says, incredulously. "Flora, it's winter. But like, also, in general, why *outside*?"

I can't help but agree with Daisy. Flora isn't exactly an outdoorsy person.

She pours herself another glass of wine before replying.

"Have I told you that I like Sebastian to chase me?" She bites her lips, looking between me and Daisy.

"*Chase* you?" I ask. "Why?"

It seems a bit of a weird thing for her to be into.

"For sex, obviously. Adds a bit of danger, you know?" Flora takes another gulp from her wine. "Anyway, I'm excited to get to do it somewhere new. Especially in such a big place."

Daisy's eyes are bugging out of her head at this information. But I actually do think I remember Flora telling me this some other time we were drunk together.

Daisy might not be, but I'm certainly interested. I wonder if I'd like being chased by a monster. It would be exhilarating, that's for sure. Certainly another thing to add to the list of reasons that I want a monster boyfriend.

Maybe I'll finally find one on this tour. We continue chatting and the wine is pretty much empty before we know it.

The bus comes to a stop, and our friendly driver lets us know that there's a shift change and that we're at a pit stop if we want to go to the store.

"Ooh yes. Let's go!" I say, hopping up out of my seat and grabbing my coat to bundle up in. I'm almost at the door when Daisy shoves a hat on my head too.

I realize a little belatedly that we must be in a monster area. The pit stop itself is deserted, but the advertisements on the filling stations all have this hunky gargoyle on them.

When we get into the store, we realize that the guys have gotten there before us. The three monsters have their arms full with snacks, tentacles too in Nereus' case.

"Have you eaten all the food we put in your bus already?" Flora jokingly asks Sebastian. He gives her a boyish shrug and it's so cute.

I get distracted looking at a package of candy with a fruit I've never seen before on it. I feel a sudden flush of warmth as Maddox sidles up next to me. He smells like sweet chestnuts, and I look to see what snack he must be carrying because it smells tasty.

"We're probably not going to stop again today." Maddox gestures to the sandwich counter behind him. "We should probably all get some sandwiches for a somewhat decent meal. You want my help ordering? It's probably different than you're used to."

"Yes please," I say, my stomach grumbling. "You guys might have been eating snacks, but we were drinking wine and gossiping, which is arguably much hungrier work."

Maddox chuckles, leading the way to the counter. He talks me through all the different sizing options, which are categorized mostly by Monster type. So I go with a safe 'witch's portion'. The fillings are slightly more straight-forward, well at least until I see crickets and abalone.

"Harpies," Maddox explains, following my gaze and the sound I must have made.

I'm proud of myself by the time we're done. Normally I might get overwhelmed with a lot of new options like that, but Maddox kept me calm through it.

Chapter 5

D^{aisy}

I thought our bus was cool, but nothing prepared me for the guys' bus.

When we were heading to our own earlier, I was so busy chatting with Flora that I didn't even spot this behemoth in the lot.

As we head inside, the color palette is a bit darker, but the layout is the same. It's just the sheer size difference that's wild, and yet the three monsters certainly fill out the space entirely. Especially Nereus, with his dark green tentacles spreading out in every direction.

It's next to Nereus that I end up when we all settle around the table to eat. Well, in between him and Sebastian. I like Sebastian, but he only has eyes for Flora, and sometimes that makes it a little difficult to form a friendship with him.

With the way Nereus has to shift his tentacles every few minutes, they brush against me. He apologizes each time it happens, and by the fourth time, I'm more annoyed about his apologies.

"It's totally fine," I tell him. "There's no need to apologize for it."

He nods at me, keeping his mouth shut tight. I can't help but laugh at him, as he was clearly trying to hold in his next apology.

Sitting next to him like this certainly gives me an opportunity to look at him closer though. He's such an interesting looking Monster, with his slippery smooth skin. He doesn't have a smidgen of hair on his head, which gives me a straight view up to the gills along the side of his head. Nereus has a flat bridge to his nose, with wide set eyes the color of the stormiest green ocean.

I look down at his tentacles again and I can't help but ask about his sitting situation.

"I'm surprised that there isn't some type of special chair for you on the bus," I gesture around at all the modifications, but then I realize that the only modification around here is *big*.

"There wouldn't be enough demand for something like that, so no one makes them." Nereus explains, continuing on when he sees my look of confusion. "There aren't very many landed monsters like me, so not much thought has gone into the design for my particular situation. I'm a musician, not an engineer, so there's only so much I can come up with myself."

Nereus chuckles and I catch a flash of his razor sharp teeth. I can't help the gulp I make at the sight of those, but he either doesn't notice or doesn't care.

I take the last bite of my sandwich before asking, "Why aren't there many landed krakens?

"It's not just krakens that I mean," he clarifies. "It's water monsters in general. They almost exclusively live in the water, and they're raised to think that water living is best."

"How did you come to live on land, then?" I hear myself asking, fascinated about the thoughts of an underwater world.

"Oh," he seems surprised that I thought to ask, his eyes widening. "Well, I'm not a full kraken. My mother is, that's for sure. But she mated a witch, and they decided to raise me on land."

"Wait, so are you part witch then?" That would be such a cool combination, I think.

Nereus nods, "I've got some water-based powers. But honestly, they're pretty crappy and using them tires me out."

I giggle, not being able to imagine Nereus getting tired at all. He always seems so rigid to me, that I can't imagine him being asleep.

"So how do water monsters live in the water then? Do they just float around?" It sounds pretty boring to me, I don't know why they wouldn't want to live on land.

Nereus' eyes light up, and I feel pulled closer to him, my knees brushing against his tentacles. "They are very secretive about what goes on down there. But my mom has told me all about it. There are underwater *cities*. I've never gotten to go to one, because they're only open to citizens."

I'm fascinated by the idea of underwater cities, but I'm also sad for this giant kraken next to me. He lives in a world that isn't prepared to accommodate him, but he's banned from the world made perfectly for him. Nereus seems lighthearted enough about it, but I'm sure there's some underlying feelings.

"I can see your pity," Nereus chuckles. "I promise it's not all bad. I love being a musician and going on tour, and I get to soak whenever I want."

Soak? "What does that mean?"

Nereus checks the empty sandwich wrapper in front of me before suggesting that he can show me if I want. Looking around at my friends, they are all deep in their own conversations. I won't be missed right now. Nodding, I decide to let the kraken take me away.

I expect Nereus to head off the bus, but instead he moves towards the back. I'm careful not to trip on any of his tentacles as I follow him.

He leads us to the back door, where I thought the end of the bus must be. But Nereus opens it into another room. The space is almost entirely filled with a giant hot tub. It has to be at least a 9ft square, and almost as deep. There's a step up into it, but even that wouldn't be high enough for me. Someone would need to lift me into it.

"How do you *fill* this on the road?" I ask, stepping up onto the step and peeking over the rim.

"We keep vats of water in a truck that they can hook up to the plumbing for me if I want. But I do need to give them notice for it."

I'm in awe of this. I know it's a simple tub, but life on the road has taught me terrible showers are the norm. Looking between Nereus and the tub, I try to imagine him in there. It's certainly designed to fit him.

The thought of him in the water like that sends a shot of pleasure right to my core. Leaning into it, I imagine what it would be like, being tangled in his tentacles in the water. What would they feel like? I've been wearing too many clothes to have felt them on my skin yet.

When I look back to Nereus, I can't help my full body shiver, goosebumps lining my limbs. His nostrils flare and he moves a little closer to me. I'm still standing on the big step, so we're almost at eye level.

I'm nervous, my fingers toying with the ends of my hair as we look at one another in silence. Nereus cups my elbow with a hand, and I swear I can feel the coolness of his skin through my sweater. He catches my gaze and I'm a goner, those stormy green eyes are so intriguing that I can't help but stare.

One of his tentacles finds the patch of skin that's showing where my socks meet my pants and he gently caresses me there. The texture is so much smoother than I could have imagined. Looking down to see it, I'm stopped in my tracks by his hand cupping my face. Nereus guides me back to his gaze.

Again, I can't help but notice his differences. Nereus' almost flat nose, his high cheekbones, his smooth lips. I realize how attractive he really is, if I push away what I've been taught about beauty. His green skin is lustrous, the color almost shifting of its own accord.

Tentatively, I reach up to touch the arm of the hand that is still tenderly cupping my face. The skin is smooth there, too, and cool to the touch. Even from my vantage on this step, Nereus still engulfs me with his sheer size.

Licking my lips, I find myself staring at his. Do I want to kiss him?

"Do you want to go back to the others?" He asks, breaking the silence.

I gulp, looking between his lips and his eyes, the vulnerability in them in this moment a new facet to this male.

"I don't know," I say, finally.

"Then you should wait until you do know." Nereus gently pulls away from me and I feel the absence of him as he moves towards the door.

I want to scream at him to come back to me, the instinct almost overwhelming. Wow, I have clearly been drinking too much wine. Since when am I like this? Nereus is right. We're on tour together, and getting into something on the first day would be a big commitment.

By the time I make it back into the main space of the bus, Nereus is already sliding back into his spot at the table.

"Where were you guys?" Maddox asks as I join him and Cleo on the couch.

"I was just showing Daisy my tub because she was curious about it." Nereus answers for me, the sound of his voice traveling up my spine in a wave of tingles.

Chapter 6

*C*leo

My heart is pounding in my chest, my breath coming unevenly as I try my best to run on the sandy terrain.

The giant minotaur is gaining on me.

Looking around, I try to find something, anything to help me. The ocean in front of me is a beacon, and I head that way.

I'm not the strongest swimmer, but surely I'm better than a minotaur.

He's almost caught up to me by the time I reach the water's edge. I don't have time to give it a second thought as I pound through the shallows.

Once I'm out of my depth, I allow myself to look back and see if I have lost him. Struggling to stay afloat through my shock, I see that the minotaur has shifted into an even bigger kraken.

My panic rises even more. I can't out swim a kraken.

Trying my best anyway, I swim further out as quickly as I can.

Something grips at my ankle, and I try to shake it off. But it's too late. He's caught me.

The tentacle drags me under the water, moving quicker than I thought possible. My back hits the sea bed as a swarm of tentacles engulf me.

Looking up, it's Nereus' face that I see, a hungry look in his gaze.

"Cleo," Nereus' face distorts.

"Babe, it's OK." Daisy's voice reaches me in my groggy state. "It was just a dream."

I hear a whimpering sound before I notice that it's coming from me. Daisy climbs in next to me, the mattress dipping a little less than normal.

Opening my eyes, it takes me a moment to remember that it's our first night on the tour bus. My view is blocked again as Daisy wraps her arms around me and pulls me into her chest.

Our legs tangle and my head is pillowed by her soft boobs. I can already feel myself drifting back to sleep.

Although my thoughts wander back to my dream. A wetness pools between my thighs as I wonder what it would *really* feel like to be wrapped in those tentacles.

Either way, I'm so comfy in Daisy's arms that it doesn't take me long to fall back to sleep.

Chapter 7

M*addox*

It's part of my pre-show ritual to find the instrument handler and make sure that my guitars are looking good. Yes, I am a little superstitious. But so are most people on the road, there's little else to entertain us when we're not on stage.

Besides, the first night on a new tour can be a logistical nightmare. Better safe than sorry.

I hear hip hop music playing and girlish laughter as I make my way past a door that's slightly ajar.

Daisy and Cleo are inside, looking like they're warming up for their set. The sight of them stops me in my tracks.

They have their hair and makeup done for the show already. Daisy's wild curls have been styled to perfection, Cleo's silky blond hair pulled up into two high pigtails.

Cleo is wearing baggy sweatpants, sitting on the floor in the splits. Her giant hoodie dwarfs her in the most adorable way.

Daisy's lithe form is visible in her leggings, her legs pure muscle as she balances on her toes. She bends forward and her loose shirt billows out, giving me a full view of her flat stomach. My mouth waters and my dick hardens at the sight.

"Oh, hey Maddox." Cleo chirps, waving at me innocently.

I open the door a little, making it seem purposeful that I had been watching them. I'm grateful it was Cleo who caught me peeping, Daisy would have seen straight through me.

"Hey," I can't help the catch in my voice. "I thought I heard music in here. Just on my way to check something but I'm sure I'll catch you later."

Pulling the door over again, I head down the hallway quickly. What the fuck is wrong with me? This isn't me. I do *not* stare at my colleagues inappropriately like that. That was a real alpha move, but I would never.

Except I did, and now my mind can't stop wandering to Daisy in that stretch. My dick is painfully hard, pressing against the tight denim of my jeans. Fuck. How am I going to deal with this?

If there was one thing that irked me about being a minotaur, it was how much fucking cum I have. I can't just give myself a quick hand job anywhere. All my blood is going to my dick, and I can't think of an option as to where I can go.

The tub. The thought strikes me and I start walking back to the lot.

I'm almost out of the building when I realize that there won't be any way to drain it. Not without asking for Nereus' help, at least.

Fuck that.

I scramble, looking around for ideas.

There's a storage closet nearby and I test the handle. Someone is looking out for me today, because the handle moves smoothly down.

The space is filled with cleaning supplies and old gig posters. I desperately pull a shelving unit in front of the door to keep it shut.

There's a stack of buckets in the corner, and I line them up. Nearly ripping open my jeans, I finally get my dick in my hands.

"Fuuuuuck," I gasp. My dick is raw and red at the top, pre-cum leaking out of the flared head. The flaps on my shaft start to pulsate, and I know it won't take me long to blow my load.

I grip myself tightly, fisting my dick and imagining Daisy's body draped over mine. My mind shifts, the picture now Daisy kneeling before me, her pale green eyes blinking up at me as she tries to fit my dick in her mouth.

Cleo materializes next to her, and they take turns sucking my dick into their mouths. Holy shit.

I groan, cum spilling from my tip at the image of Cleo's bright blue eyes starting into mine as she licks my dick like a lollipop.

My eyes fly open and I almost miss the first bucket. I spill my load, pretending it's over the girls faces and chests. It's an effort to stay quiet.

After I fill nearly three buckets, I'm finally spent. Resting my head against the cool stone wall, I wonder what the fuck just happened.

Quickly tidying up the room, I right myself to normal and sneak back out of the storage closet.

The clock on the wall shows me that I've run out of time to find the instrument handler. Now I'd just be getting in his way.

If I didn't already feel unsettled, I certainly do now.

One of the stage crew members asks me a question, and now I'm stuck here answering questions to a group of three of them.

I feel a familiar presence behind me, Nereus' voice filling my head as he whispers to me.

"If you needed help, you should have asked. I would have happily obliged."

He can't mean what I think he means, right?

I'm grateful for my fur when I feel the blush forming on my neck and cheeks.

Normally, I can handle Nereus' little jibes and flirtations fine. But today is not a normal day for some reason. My dick swells in my pants again and I shift to adjust it. How did he even know?

Not for the first time, I wonder what those tentacles would feel like, wrapped around my dick. The thought makes me even harder and I stumble a bit from the dizzying feeling.

Nereus is quick to catch me, his hands gripping my shoulders.

"You feeling OK?" He asks me, trying to turn me around to face him. "I didn't really mean to rile you up again."

I huff, shame filling me. Storming off, I refuse to look at him to see him laughing at me.

Maybe I need to head for that storage closet again.

Chapter 8

*N*ereus

I'm not sure what to do. Maddox has stormed off and I feel like an asshole.

Staring after the fuming minotaur, I try to decide if I should follow him or not. This isn't normally how Maddox would react if I made a jibe like that.

We make fun of each other all the time. Fuck, I consistently make innuendos at Maddox's expense. It's one of the only ways for me to take the edge off the fact that my mate doesn't want to be mated. I didn't realize they were annoying him this much.

Do they, though? He normally acts coy and bashful when I do it, not storming off like this. He never acts like this, and he especially doesn't get this aroused by it. There's definitely something else going on here that I'm missing.

Fuck it. I decide to follow him. For his own safety, if anything.

I could smell the scent of his cum all over him when I found him chatting to the crew. I was only thinking to tease him a little, not set him off on a rampage.

Catching up to Maddox is a lot quicker than it should be. I find him standing in a hallway, staring into a room through a gap in the door. A glance in shows me a very attractive scene of Daisy and Cleo warming up together. Daisy helping Cleo ease into a stretch.

Maddox's hand moves towards his crotch, and I grip him by the wrist before he does anything stupid.

"What the fuck do you think you're doing?" I hiss, pulling him away. I flip him around and press him up against the wall.

My body presses against the length of him, trapping Maddox in place.

"Maddox, what the fuck?" I hiss at him again, seething. "Those are your colleagues."

It's almost as if Maddox shakes himself out of a daze, tilting his head as his eyes seem to focus on me. He's not going into heat is he? I press my hand against his forehead, but his temperature is normal. Sniffing his amber and pine scent, there isn't any trace of a shift there.

Maddox is limp beneath me, and he lets out a soft little omega whine. Fuck, I can't resist that sound.

I try to think fast on my feet. Flora and Sebastian are doing a walk through on the stage right now, and the girls are in there, so there shouldn't be anyone on the bus.

"Follow me," I alpha bark at Maddox. It's not something that I like to do, but I can't dawdle. I need to help my mate before we're due on stage.

Making quick work of the walk to the bus, Maddox follows behind. We get a few strange looks from workers, but we don't draw too much attention.

Thankfully, the bus is empty when we get there.

"Clothes off and into the tub." I direct Maddox, dipping into my bunk to grab some lube.

When I join him in the tub room, I can't help but stare at Maddox's cock. It's unlike anything I've seen before. There's a ring, mid way down that looks rigid. From that ring all the way to his flared tip are little flaps that swell and pulsate.

My own cock is hard at the sight of Maddox in the tub waiting for me, his cock in his hand.

I can't waste any time though. I strip off my shirt, tossing it into the pile of clothes that we need to keep clean for later. Before getting into the tub, I double check the lock on the door.

When I finally climb in, Maddox is palming his cock, watching me. His honey brown eyes are glazed over with lust.

"Come here," I say. Maddox wastes no time, his hooves delicately stepping over my tentacles. I wrap him in my arms, pressing his muzzle against my chest.

"I didn't mean to work you up like this," I tell him, stroking his back soothingly. Maddox shivers from the contact, nodding against me.

"I know that," he says. "I just don't know what's wrong with me. I was walking by, and the girls were stretching and they looked so *good*. I couldn't help myself, I had to cum so bad."

I replace Maddox's hand with my own, feeling the pulsating flares against my palm. Stroking him gently, Maddox lets out a deep and guttural sound that goes straight to my groin.

"That's it. Good boy," I say as he relaxes into my embrace a little bit more.

"Was that the second time you were looking at them then?" I ask, worried about whatever mess Maddox might have gotten himself into.

He nods against my chest, "I came in a broom closet like a fucking teenager."

I can't help the chortle of surprise that escapes me at that.

"Wow. That's a choice," I say. "Don't worry about it now. Just relax." I continue stroking his back with one hand and his cock with the other. "I've got you. This doesn't have to mean anything. Just a friend helping a friend, OK?"

I reassure him, only because I know that Maddox will get in his head about this later. He has such an aversion to any kind of sexual encounter with an alpha.

Maddox nods his head before shifting up and nuzzling into the crook of my neck.

I try to stay impartial to the experience of having him here in my arms. But I can't help the contentedness that flows through me, having my warm mate pressed against me like this.

I need to focus though, we can't spend too much time away from the venue before someone will come looking for us. I use my tentacles to spread some lube on one. They're slippery enough, but I want to make sure that this is an easy experience for Maddox.

Letting go of his cock for a minute to spread his ass wide, I'm met with an even more desperate whine than earlier.

"One second, baby." I use a tentacle to move his tail out of the way, my hands spreading his cheeks. "That's it, good boy. Just relax." I soothe him as I slowly ease a tentacle inside him, pressing against his sensitive spot.

Fuck, that feels so good, the tight grip of his warm hold around my tentacle. I relax my grip on him and reach back down to stroke his cock again.

I make quick work of making my omega cum. He tenses around me, gripping my shoulders tight as his face presses against my neck. I wish I could spend longer doing this, to enjoy this over hours, making him cum multiple times.

Keeping a firm press on Maddox's prostate, I massage his balls to milk him dry. Once he is spent, he fully collapses on me with his full weight, whimpering and shivering.

"Fuck. I'm so, so sorry." Maddox whispers.

"Shh," I stroke his back again. "It's alright. Just a friend helping a friend."

Chapter 9

Daisy

My grin is wide, sweat pouring down my back as I hold my final pose. I always struggle to calm my breathing at this point in the performance.

"Give it up for my amazing dancers!" Flora shouts into the mic. The crowd goes wild for me and Cleo, and my grin becomes a little more genuine.

We can't properly see the crowds during our performances, and I kind of like it that way. So far the monster audiences have been a little less receptive than the human ones.

I continue to hold my pose until the lights go off. Cleo and I have six seconds to get off stage at that point, so it's always a mad rush around the set.

"Third show done!" Cleo squeals, running towards me when we make it off.

I go in for a kiss on the cheek, but Cleo moves her head slightly and our lips brush before I can pull away.

"Oops!" Cleo giggles, laughing off my mishap and we continue to have a mini dance party with our post-performance high.

Well, at least I try to. But I can't help thinking about how good that slight kiss was. Why do I want to go in for another?

I do my best to shrug it off, tugging Cleo out of the way of the crew. Nereus and Maddox are waiting side stage, probably to listen and watch before they're due to go on.

Maddox stares off to the side, avoiding my gaze and clenching his jaw. He's been acting super weird since our first performance. I'm starting to feel a bit self-conscious about it at this point. Did he not like our dancing or something? It's not like he hasn't seen us in rehearsals before.

I decide to lie to myself and pretend that it must be something else.

Nereus, on the other hand, gives me a big grin over his crossed arms. His muscles flex a little and I blush under his attention.

I still haven't really processed how I feel about him since that first day on the bus, but we've all been super busy getting to grips with the new routine. I've seen him in passing a few times since then, and he's been super friendly each time. The problem is, he has been just as friendly with Cleo. Was he flirting with me? Or worse, was he flirting with both of us?

"Let's go grab a drink and watch the rest of the show!" Cleo exclaims. So instead of going over and talking to him, I just wave in Nereus' direction and follow Cleo to our dressing room.

"If we're quick, we might catch the end of Flora's set." I tell Cleo as we change out of our costumes and touch up our makeup.

That puts Cleo in gear. We change and get to the VIP bar in record time to watch the rest of the show.

Chapter 10

M*addox*

God, I look like such a fucking asshole at the moment. But I am struggling with my primal, basal instincts around Daisy and Cleo.

It looked like a mishap when they kissed coming off stage, but the way they were jumping together was too much for me to look at.

I genuinely can't look at Daisy right now without getting a crazy hard on. Luckily, I haven't needed Nereus' help again.

Surprisingly, the giant kraken has been acting completely normal since *that* happened. So I'm not feeling too awkward about it at least.

Well, except that Nereus has been a little bit nicer lately. Although that seems to be aimed more towards the girls. I would almost think that he's flirting with them, except he's been just as nice to Flora.

Sebastian walks by me and Nereus, getting ready to join Flora on stage. "Lighten up a bit, friend." He says, clapping me on the shoulder. Fuck, he's right. I put on a brave face, pretending that my head isn't in full turmoil at the moment.

At least I can relax and watch the show. It's been a real pleasure to watch Flora and Sebastian perform together these past couple nights.

More importantly, I've been enjoying watching Flora's set and the girls dancing. The only time I've really been able to watch Daisy and Cleo lately is during their set. My dick can at least stay calm for most of it. But that's because I'm starstruck with how good they are at working a crowd, Flora too.

There are definitely some monsters who have come to these shows skeptical about the human performance, but they are won over by the time the dancers leave the stage.

I specifically spoke to the venue staff to make sure that the house lights stayed as low as possible during their performance. That way the girls couldn't see whether or not the audience was engaged.

I'm not sure how things are going to go down when we have our first performance in a human area tomorrow.

Chapter 11

Cleo

I point my toes, feeling the stretch through my hamstrings as I bend forward. My ankles are cushioned by my borrowed leg warmers. Not that Daisy has noticed that I took them yet. She's hyper vigilant this evening, not fully relaxing into any of her stretches.

"What's wrong with you?" I finally ask her.

"Don't you think that the vibes are really off here?" She replies with a huff, looking back again to the closed door of the dance studio.

I think back to getting to this venue, nodding to Daisy. The staff here certainly haven't been as friendly. But tonight is our first show at a human venue, so I had expected things to be a little different.

It wasn't a huge surprise to me that the humans were being rude to the monsters. But what was surprising was how rude they were to us, too.

"You seem scared," I say, moving to kneel next to my friend. "Nobody has done anything bad, just been a little standoffish."

"I know, I know." Daisy sighs, putting her head in my chest. I stroke her back, knowing not to touch her perfectly styled curls. Though I wish I could play with them, I wish I could bury my hands in her hair.

"I just..." Daisy continues. "I think I felt more safe in the monster venues."

Flora and Sebastian work so well on stage together, despite their aesthetic differences. She wears a purple wig, along with matching heeled boots and a sparkly silver dress. Sebastian wears all black, his sleeves rolled up to play his guitar, and I can't help but appreciate his forearms on display like that. He keeps his wings out while he performs and the shimmering black and green looks so cool in the stage lighting.

Our set with Flora went great, the crowd was super engaged and it was so much fun. Daisy and I have taken to the VIP bar again. Watching the rest of the show from up here is such a cool experience. It's not like anything I've been able to do before this tour.

The audience seems pretty into Flora, that's for sure. They scream as she says goodbye and the stage goes dark for the guys to set up their set.

A few groups of people towards the back of the crowd seem to be leaving, but they could always be taking a break. More people leave while the set is being changed, more than normal for a bathroom break.

"Are they all leaving?" I ask Daisy who is standing next to me.

"Maybe they're just taking a break," she strokes my back as she says it. I'm not stupid, despite what some people might think, and I can see right through her. She's definitely just trying to reassure me. Daisy nibbles at her plush pink lip, taking some of her lip gloss off.

"Here," I pass her mine to top up.

It only takes a few minutes before Nereus is coming out on stage to a little less cheers than normal. I scream louder to make up for it. Maddox is much the same, but the crowd seems a bit more engaged when Sebastian comes out.

The audience does get into the music though as the guys start to play, so that's good.

I can't help but get distracted by Maddox as he plays his bass, his long fingers expertly plucking the strings. The way the light is hitting his white fur, I can see all the muscles in his arms clearly.

Nereus is a distraction too. He could probably play every single drum in front of him at once if he wanted to with all his tentacles and arms.

Looking at Nereus reminds me of my dream, how it felt to be trapped by his tentacles and held down. It's weird to admit to myself that I was really into it. Even thinking about it now is getting me all worked up.

I need to get this out of my system. Surely there's someone in this bar I could get with tonight to help take the edge off. A quick glance around the room doesn't give me hope, but there are two guys that have been eyeing up me and Daisy.

Fuck it. I give them a flirty smile, flicking my hair back and turning to face Daisy again, showing them my back.

"Did you call them over?" Daisy asks, knowing the situation right away. She downs her drink as I nod in confirmation.

Like clockwork, the two guys make their way over to us. They place their drinks on our table and make their introductions. I barely pay any attention, nodding and smiling when I'm supposed to.

"Do you want to come back to the bus for an after party?" I ask the one closest to me, placing my hand on his arm and fluttering my lashes.

Daisy checks with Flora at the bar that she's cool with a party and before we know it, Flora is in planning mode. She may be mated now, but Flora is still a party girl at heart.

The party is going to be on the guys' bus to accommodate our monster guests. Perfect, Daisy and I will be able to sneak away with these guys easily.

Chapter 12

Nereus

Maddox and I sit at our table on the bus, beers in hand as a group of human women talk to us. Maddox is carrying the team, chatting to them all, but I can't help but be distracted by Daisy and Cleo.

There is a pair of slimy looking human men hanging off the girls. I can't help but instantly dislike them. I have to grit my teeth to stay in my seat when Cleo starts to get a bit more handsy in her flirting.

"Can I touch one?" A shrill voice asks from beside me.

"What?" I look down to see her hand is on the way to one of my tentacles. "No."

I shut her down, her hand frozen in mid air.

"Oh, sorry." She quickly moves away, going to the dance floor to chat to some other monster.

At least she's freed up my access to the girls if I need.

The guy chatting to Daisy is touching her arm more when they talk, and my stomach churns. She isn't his to touch. Daisy pulls him up to dance with her, the idiot just standing there swaying while she does all the dancing.

Not that I'd be any better at dancing with her. Tentacles weren't exactly conducive to pretty dancing. That's why I prefer to play drums and not guitar on stage.

The human man starts to cup Daisy's waist and ass as she dances. His hand catches on the hem of her shimmering gold dress, nearly putting her full ass on display. My muscles groan with the effort to stay in my seat.

Daisy stumbles a little here and there, clearly too drunk to properly be consenting to this. I have been nursing this one drink all night to keep an eye on my friends, and I'm trying to decide if I should intervene or not. The guy takes

Daisy's hand, gesturing toward the door, she nods with a flirty smile.

I'm halfway out of my seat when she looks back to Cleo. My eyes follow her gaze to see Cleo looking horrified at the guy she is with. It looks like she's arguing with him, telling him to leave, if I'm understanding properly. Either way, she needs my help.

"Do we have a problem here?" I ask, raising myself up to my full height, my head nearly touching the top of the bus.

The human man sinks back in his seat. Coward.

"I want him to leave and he won't." Cleo says to me. Her look is pleading, definitely asking for my help.

I give the guy one more look and he scampers, taking his friend with him and leaving Daisy confused in the middle of the group of dancers. Once she recovers from her shock, Daisy rushes over to Cleo, who is already crying.

Covering the girls from view with my body, I gesture to Sebastian to get his attention. I motion for him to cut the music. Sebastian takes one glance at Cleo and steals the attention. I shift to cover them better.

"Party's over." Sebastian calls out in a loud, booming voice.

No one will argue with his alpha bark like that in his own space. The crowd disperses quickly and once the last straggler leaves, Maddox checks the bathroom and gives the all clear. Sebastian shuts and locks the front door.

"What's going on?" Flora asks, moving towards me.

I move out of her way so she can see and get to her friends. Gesturing to the guys, we move down to the back of the bus to give the girls some privacy.

Well, maybe the illusion of privacy. The three of us stay quiet to listen in.

"What happened?" Sebastian hisses.

"Some guy did something to Cleo and she wanted him out. So I made sure he left but then she started crying, and I didn't think she deserved an audience for that." I say quickly, trying to listen in.

I can hear Flora and Daisy's voices the most, but every few seconds Cleo hiccups through her tears. I can just make out that the guy was making fun of some monsters and Cleo told him to leave.

"Then," Cleo hiccups again. "He said he was more en-titled to me than any monster guy was."

"What the fuck?" Flora says loudly.

"No, it's OK." Cleo continues. "Nereus stepped in then and I'm just being a little dramatic anyway, I'm sure. We didn't need to stop the party."

"Oh, babe," Daisy soothes. "Of course we needed to stop the party. It's not fun unless we're all having fun, right?"

I can't hear the rest of what they say for a minute. Daisy really does look out for Cleo, but she doesn't seem to have anyone looking out for her. Maybe I can be that.

Not that Daisy has acted on anything since our encounter on the first day. But I don't need anything back from her in order to be nice. To treat her well and show her what it's like to be the one looked after. She takes on so much for Cleo to protect her.

"Fuck, I shouldn't have left you alone." I hear Daisy saying, putting the blame on herself.

"I knew they were creeps," Cleo replies. "But I just wanted to let off some steam, you know? And it would've been fun if he hadn't opened his stupid mouth."

I struggle to hold in my laugh at that one.

"Come on, babe," Daisy says. "Let's just go to bed."

I take that as my cue to come out of the shadows. "I'll walk you," I find myself volunteering.

Cleo sniffles again, nodding. Flora says goodbye to Sebastian, stating that she wants to spend the night with her girls. Flora has stayed with us the past few nights, the first night being torture for her to sleep on her own apparently.

I did grumble a bit initially about her staying with us, but I also wasn't surprised.

Walking the girls a few minutes to the bus, Flora hangs back with me as Daisy has her arm around Cleo as they walk. Their friendship really is beautiful, all three of them, but Daisy and Cleo specifically. I had gathered from rehearsal for the tour that they lived together, too.

That has me thinking about my own home and my pond. I do miss getting to go into the water every night.

Flora gently pats me on the arm, "Thank you for stepping in." The girls all wave and say their thanks as they get into the bus and shut the door behind them.

I wait a moment, looking around to see how safe it is out here. There's no one else out, and I realize that I might be being a little overbearing, so I turn to leave.

There's a clicking noise behind me. My head whips around on high alert, but it's the door to the bus. Daisy is climbing out, clicking it shut behind her.

"Hey," she says, walking quickly towards me. "I just—I wanted to say thank you, for earlier. Cleo is my world and it's nice to know that there's someone else looking out for her."

Her wording is strange, is she claiming Cleo as a partner?

Daisy moves closer to me, tip toeing around my tentacles. She lifts her hands to my chest, her warm fingers brushing against the well worn fabric of my t-shirt.

I hold my breath, hardly daring to wonder what she will do next. Daisy's hands fist in my t-shirt, pulling me down so I bend at the waist. I think she's trying to lower my head to hers, but it doesn't get quite that far.

"You're so damn tall," Daisy laughs, leaning up onto her toes. I help her out a bit, lowering myself on my tentacles some more, curling them around her legs.

"That better?" I ask, now at her height.

She giggles, cupping my face in her hands. They feel so tiny against me.

"Am I reading this wrong?" she asks me, leaning closer so that our lips almost touch.

I finally give back some energy, now that I understand fully what she's going for. My hand finds her waist, my other her cheek, pulling her closer into a gentle kiss.

Her scent envelopes me, black cherries and allspice, perfect on this cold winter night. I wasn't sure before, or rather, I hardly dared to believe it.

Mate.

When she doesn't pull away, I try again. This time I flick my tongue against her lips.

Daisy gasps, leaning back. I loosen my hold on her, worried that I've done something wrong.

"You good?" I ask.

"Yeah," her eyes are wide. "I just wasn't expecting your tongue to feel like *that*."

I stick out my tongue with a smile, the tiny little textured nubs visible to her. Stupidly, I hadn't thought to warn her that it might be a little different. If I was full kraken, they would be little teeth, and she might not be a fan of those.

"I—I'm sorry," she stammers a little as I put my tongue back in my mouth. "I really haven't been with any monster males yet, and I didn't think to expect that."

I can't help but chuckle. "It's OK, sweetheart."

Pulling her closer to me again, I take the time to brush her wild curls away from her face.

"Wanna try that again?" I ask.

She eagerly comes to me for another kiss. Daisy gasps at the contact and I use the opportunity to explore her further.

Her mouth is soft and delicate, her body warm and inviting. Daisy's omega scent blossoms for me, the cloves in it coming to the surface. It's intoxicating. I groan against her mouth, pulling her even closer.

Daisy's hands start to roam, feeling my body as I do the same for her. I can't help but move my touch across her graceful form, her firm ass.

She reluctantly breaks our kissing, pulling back and looking towards the bus, her expression torn.

I make the decision for her, raising back up to my usual height.

"Go look after Cleo," I say.

"I guess I'll see you tomorrow, then."

She makes quick work of getting back into the bus and I watch her to make sure she gets in OK.

Daisy glances back with a smile before clicking the door shut.

Chapter 13

Daisy

I smile at Nereus one last time, clicking the door shut behind me.

Holy shit.

My back presses against the door, my breathing erratic as I try to piece together what just happened. I can't believe I just did that.

Fuck, it felt so good though. My panties are dripping from the memory of his rough tongue against mine. His cocky laugh when he realized what was happening. *Did that really just happen?*

"Everything OK?" Flora's voice breaks me from my thoughts. "You were gone a while. I was just about to go looking for you. Could you not find Nereus?"

I blink at Flora, my mind taking a second to catch up.

"I found him alright."

Flora searches my eyes, "is everything OK?"

"Yeah," I decide to spill the beans. "Umm... so, Nereus and I made out and it was really good and I think I'm into him. I don't want to say anything to Cleo about it though because she's upset and—"

"OMG!" Flora squeals. "Cleo's not upset. She's eating chips and watching Bravo, you know how she recovers quickly."

Flora jumps in her spot, her excitement obvious and I am still struggling to keep up. My mind is still tangled up in those tentacles.

"What's all the commotion about?" Cleo chirps, sauntering up to us in the entryway.

"Oh, you know, *nothing*... except, hmm... what was that, Daisy?" Flora teases me.

My grin starts to form, finally feeding off Flora's energy. "I made out with Nereus..."

Cleo's squeal is even louder than Flora's, "What?! Oh hell I am so *jealous*, he's so hot!"

We move into the living space, getting settled on the couch. I take over Cleo's bowl of chips as I catch the girls up on what happened.

"Wait," Flora says. "So where did this all come from? I doubt you just randomly kissed?"

"Oh! So yeah, we had this hot almost kiss thing on the first day of tour when he was showing me the tub."

"I *thought* you guys spent ages in there!" Cleo chips in.

"The sexual chemistry is just *there*," I tell them. "I really can't help myself when we're alone like that."

"Ugh, I totally get it." Cleo sighs dramatically, popping a chip into her mouth. "Well, not the sexual chemistry part, I don't think I've ever been alone in a room with him. But oh, I had this dream about him catching me in those tentacles and wow, I need to know what that feels like."

"I'm curious about those tentacles too..." Flora leads, trying to get me to bite. It's honestly not that hard.

"OK, so like he's wrapped up my legs in them, but my stupid *clothes* were in the way. But God, I can only imagine..." I clear my throat. "It's like a really firm embrace, but everywhere all at once. It's so good."

We giggle and chat about some of the other monsters we've met, staying up late.

Chapter 14

Maddox

Nereus finally opens the door to the bus. Sebastian and I are drinking a beer at the table, having already cleaned the bus up.

"That took you a while," I say, leaning back in my seat.

Sebastian nods as he takes a sip of his beer. I swear that I can almost see a blush form on Nereus' cheeks as he shrugs.

"Took a while to tuck them all in, you know?" Nereus moves to join us at the table. The look on Sebastian's face is what sets me over the edge into a fit of laughter.

"I know you are joking," Sebastian sighs. "But please give me a break over here. It's hard enough being away from Flora."

"And that's why I never want to be mated." I exclaim, taking a sip of my beer. God, I'm reminded again as to why I wouldn't want an alpha. Someone being that obsessed with me would be torture.

"I'm going to take a soak." Nereus says, abruptly shoving out of his seat and storming to the back of the bus.

"What's his problem?" Sebastian asks.

I just shrug. I don't know why everyone always expects me to be some kind of Nereus translator.

Sebastian starts to scroll on his phone, most likely texting Flora.

My mind starts to wander to the girls who I was talking to earlier at the party. They were all so pretty, and all very willing to get with me. But I just wasn't getting turned on the way I used to at these kinds of things.

Daisy's dancing on the other hand... before everything went down, I couldn't take my eyes off her. Holy fuck I was turned on by that. I was dumbfounded watching her, if Daisy had turned her attention on me, I think I would have cum in my pants. I'm barely hanging on right now because of the alcohol dimming my nervous system. And Nereus just took over the tub.

I don't want to be feeling like this, hard as fuck every time I see Daisy, even with Cleo too. But I can't help it. I want to be able to give them my attention, to dote on them both, but that was getting more and more difficult. I know that they've noticed my change in behavior too, and the last thing I want to do is push either of them away.

Sebastian chokes on his beer, coughing hard and staring at his phone.

"What is it?" I ask, stepping up and clapping him on the back. Sebastian tries to shrug it off, but with the angle I see what's on the screen. Five words stand out.

Daisy made out with Nereus.

Sebastian locks his phone quickly. "Dude. Shit, you shouldn't have seen that. Flora is going to go crazy when I tell her you saw that."

I huff, fuming. It's difficult to hold myself back from tearing at the floor with my hoof.

Nereus knew that I was into Daisy. How could he do this to me?

I don't know whether to confront him in the tub, or get into my bunk.

"I'm going for a run." I tell Sebastian, tossing off my shirt and heading outside.

Chapter 15

C*leo*

A buzzing, vibrating sensation fills my body, and I wake in a panic. Luckily, it only takes me a second to realize that the bus engine has just been turned on.

After I make sense of that, I notice that my head is in someone's lap, their hand in my hair. Daisy's spicy, fruity smell fills my nose and I relax against her.

I snuggle back in, content to stay here as the bus begins to move. Usually when the bus is in motion it lulls me to sleep, but it's not working today.

Memories from last night come at me. I push aside the interactions with the creepy guy, instead focusing on being here with the girls.

Daisy and Nereus making out... that was probably a sight to behold. I wonder what she looked like, tangled in his tentacles, wrapped in his arms. His smoky green skin against her fiery red hair.

Did he even wrap her up in his tentacles? I think I remember her saying he did. I wonder if he ran his fingers through her delicate curls? Probably not, Daisy hates it when her hair is touched. She's let me play with it a few times, before she's due to wash it or if we're not going out anywhere.

I'm kind of obsessed with her hair, especially up close. From a distance it looks like pure amber, but up close there are peach and blond tones. I love that some strands are almost a pink color.

Daisy's hand is resting in my own hair right now. I must have fallen asleep with her stroking it. That's always a quick way for me to drift off. This isn't the first time I've woken up like this, although normally we don't make it through the full night.

It was sweet of her to comfort me, even if I don't re-member the context. I do love how Daisy dotes on me, and I think that she likes to have someone to look after. I feel so safe in her arms.

I've never had a friendship come even close to what I have with Daisy, Flora included. When my mom passed, Daisy and her dad were there to help me. They let me move in with them while I got set up on my own.

The glowing street lights flash in the window as the bus drives past them. So while it might feel like morning, I do my best to close my eyes and rest some more.

Daisy

The pain in my neck is the first thing I feel. My head is tipped back on the back of the couch, resting against the hard wood of the wall.

Nice. If I had shifted forward just a little bit, this would have been much more comfortable.

The weight in my lap reminds me why I decided not to move, clearly not wanting to disturb Cleo in her sleep.

I look down to see her messy blond hair draped over me, the rest of her body curled into a ball.

"Morning," Flora says, walking into the main living space where Cleo and I slept. "You girls were too cute together, I just couldn't bring myself to wake you up."

"My neck doesn't thank you," I say. It comes out grumpier than I mean it to. "At least we don't have a show tonight."

I lean forward a little, trying to rub out the crick in my neck. The shift wakes up Cleo, who yawns and stretches like a little kitten. It's far too adorable for my grumpy state. I playfully flick her on the shoulder.

"My body is so sore you little brat, thanks for falling asleep on me." I tease.

Cleo just giggles, asking when we are going to stop for a coffee.

Chapter 16

Daisy

Our coffee time ended up taking much longer than expected. The bus was on a trajectory that meant we had a few more hours before we were allowed to stop.

I at least got to take a little nap in my bunk to help with my neck pain.

We have a day off today, and while the others decided to spend their time at the National Park, Daisy and I decided to do what we do best. Shopping.

Our first call was obviously our coffees, and now that we had them in hand it was time for some good old window shopping. We can't exactly buy much, with the limited space on the bus. Actually, Cleo will probably just see that as a challenge to only buy skimpy clothes.

Speaking of, I'm nearly dragged by Cleo to the nearest lingerie store. I'm promised that we're just *looking*. Which means that we will be leaving here with at least a few new pieces. I've learned to just go along with it.

I busy myself, looking at the cosmetics and spraying a couple perfumes. Some of them smell like an artificial version of Cleo's natural vanilla cake scent.

Cleo will go and pick out what we're trying on, that's usually how this works. She has been picking out my clothes for me for at least the last five years. I think it's cute how she likes to play dress up with me. Sometimes we're even in matching outfits, but most of the time they're at least coordinating. I especially don't mind if it makes Cleo happy.

Besides, she dresses me way better than I'd dress myself.

Cleo comes bounding up to me in a ball of energy, a pile of garments in hand. We sneak into the same dressing room while the attendant isn't looking, as we usually do. We stopped being shy about changing around one another a long time ago. Dancing does that to you.

"Let's start with these," Cleo says, holding up two very skimpy pieces.

I thought we'd be trying on pajama sets, not sexy lingerie. Not only that, but they're matching blue and green sets.

"To match our eyes!" Cleo says.

I just laugh, stripping down to my underwear, she can be a little wild at times. The dark, moody green of the piece is hardly the same color as my eyes, but it does remind me of a certain Kraken's.

Cleo's, on the other hand, is a royal blue that matches her piercing eyes perfectly. I turn to see that she has hers on already.

"What do you think?" she asks, turning off to show her ass and back. The piece is pretty much backless, different straps crisscrossing over her pale skin. There isn't much of a bottom to it either, the slip of a g-string barely visible between her cheeks.

I can't help but gulp, my pussy growing slick at the sight. I've always been a little bit attracted to Cleo... I mean, who wouldn't be? She's beautiful.

But seeing her like this is opening a whole other trove of feelings. I'm still in my own underwear, and it's a good thing, because I would have ruined anything else with the state my pussy is currently in.

I stalk a little closer to Cleo in the tiny space. Leaning down the slight inch or two in the difference of our height to whisper in her ear.

"You look so hot right now," I trail a finger down her arm gently. "And it's got me wondering why I've never seen you like this before."

Cleo lets out a little whimper, bucking against my hip.

I step back, a bit unsure of my new found confidence and my developed attraction. Cleo stares at me open mouthed as I put my clothes back on and sit on the little stool in the corner.

"Try on the rest of what you picked," I tell her, leaning back in my chair to enjoy the show.

Cleo blinks at me, a slow smile forming on her lips. "OK," she says.

She tries on the two sets of pajamas that she picked up. Both are revealing, her ass hanging out of them. Her full stomach is on display with the crop top on one set.

When Cleo gets dressed back into her own clothes, I get up to leave the room.

"But you didn't try yours on," Cleo says with a pout.

"I know they'll fit me. You picked them."

I pick up all the clothes, striding to the register to pay.

Chapter 17

Maddox

I had already signed up to this stupid trip to the National Park, so now I was stuck here.

Flora and Sebastian just said their goodbyes, Nereus having teased them relentlessly on the way here. It was pretty clear to us all that they were here for some chasing and fucking.

Nereus pulls out his phone, taking a look at the maps app.

"There's a pretty big pond here that I want to check out. You down?" He asks.

I shrug. I'm pissed off that I got stuck with Nereus today. I should have gone shopping with the girls. That would have been fun, except for the minor detail that we were solidly in human territory. I could hardly just be a lone minotaur, traipsing around.

So my options had been to stay in the bus alone all day, or join Nereus in the park. Whilst we hadn't been on tour that long yet, I knew that cabin fever would set in quicker if I was stuck on the bus for a day off. Plus, the fresh air would do me good.

I look back to where Flora and Sebastian should be, but there's no one there. Something catches my peripheral though, and I see Sebastian in his dragon form. He flies low to the trees with Flora on his back.

"He better be careful not to get caught doing that," Nereus chuckles.

"And so what?" I say. "They'll be fine. I'd like to see some human try it on with Sebastian over it."

My tone is snappy, and Nereus picks up on it.

"What's up with you today?" He asks me, his voice sounding genuinely concerned. I know that's a lie, why is he even bothering to pretend to care?

"Nothing."

We walk in silence, eventually making it to the pond that Nereus described. It's picturesque, with clusters of irises bordering and in the water. There's even a few lily pads with sleeping frogs under cover.

I finally relax, breathing in the air and realizing that I'm far away from the hustle of the cities we've been traveling to. I can just exist and roam.

Nereus heads off into the water, so I do my best to ignore him. I take a sniff of the air, ignoring the salt water smell of Nereus that is definitely not part of this landscape.

It's in my nature to want to roam like this. Taking a wander and seeing what hidden pieces of wildlife I can find.

By the time I loop fully around the pond, the sun is high in the sky and I am warm under my fur.

"Come to the water, it's much cooler." Nereus calls from his spot, floating near the banks.

There's a tiny dock, and I am in need of a quick, cool dunk. I huff a little sigh, my fur will take ages to dry after this. A glance at the sky shows no incoming clouds, so hopefully that will help.

I strip off my clothes and lower myself into the water from the dock. It's not as cold as I expect, especially for this time of year. It's warmer in here than it was out there.

"Hmm," I huff.

"I lied," Nereus says, moving closer to me. "There's definitely some sort of hot spring further in, but it's a nice temperature here.

"I just wanted to get you in the water with me," he adds.

"Not the first thing you've lied about recently." I huff again, my septum ring moving with the force of it.

"What?" He sounds surprised.

"I know what happened last night, and I'm pissed that you would do that when you knew I was into her." His stormy gaze meets mine, but I'm not backing down on this.

"*Are* you into her?" Nereus asks. "Because from where I'm standing, you've been objectifying her and treating her like shit."

My tail curls between my legs at his words. He's right, I'm being an asshole.

"She and I have been toeing the line since the first day of tour," Nereus continues. "Not that it's any of your busi-ness. It's not my fault that you couldn't control yourself."

I forget that I'm in Nereus' territory before it's too late. Tentacles wrap around me, trapping me in place. Nereus looks right into my gaze as I struggle in his grip. I can't get myself free.

Stomping my hoof in the mud in frustration, that privilege gets taken from me too. Nereus lifts me so that my hooves no longer touch the pond floor.

I'm completely at his mercy, submerged in a mass of water and tentacles.

"I don't want to be like that," I admit.

"Then let me help you blow off some more steam, then." Nereus suggests, moving a tentacle teasingly against my ass cheeks. "Then you might be able to hold it together long enough to get her attention in the way that you want."

I can't help the low whine that escapes me. My dick grows heavy and long as Nereus toys with my ass.

"What do you say, *omega*? Do you need this tentacle in your ass?"

I whine again, bucking in his grip.

"You have to tell me you want it this time," Nereus says. "You have to tell me you want *me* this time."

The little whine escapes me yet again and I don't know what to do. I want Nereus, but I don't want to commit to an alpha in the way that he is asking.

Nereus teases the ring of my asshole, waiting for my response. When it doesn't come, he relaxes his grip, pulling away from me.

"Wait." I hear my voice saying. "I want you Nereus."

He sets me down so that my hooves can touch the bed of the pond again, his grip tightening on me as his stormy green gaze searches mine.

"Are you sure?" He asks. The vulnerability in his softening gaze is something I've never seen from him before. Nereus leans closer, his eyes searching mine.

"I'm sure." I press my muzzle against his mouth, nudging him a little to ask for access.

Nereus opens up for me and I explore his mouth with my tongue. I've always been so curious as to how those little nubs would feel, and they send tingles down my spine.

His tentacle finally pushes into my asshole and I groan loudly against him. He shoves in, inch by inch, and I have to pull away from our kiss, my breath coming out in little pants.

"That's it. Good boy," Nereus' words sent a bolt of pleasure straight to my dick.

He continues kissing me, moving down my muzzle and cheek, alternating between that and licking my fur with his ribbed tongue.

His kisses make their way down my chest, and he pulls my nipple ring into his mouth, sucking harshly. I cry out at the sharp pain, but the pleasure that follows is worth it. His attentions are sending shivers down my spine and my dick bucks against nothing but water.

Nereus submerges his head and gives my dick the attention it needs. He sucks my head into his mouth, the pleasure concentrating there almost painfully. That is until his hands wrap around my shaft, balancing out the sensations.

He continues his onslaught, bringing me closer to the edge along with his tentacle in my ass.

I feel like I'm going to explode.

Telling Nereus to pull away, he just doubles down. He sucks harder, moving his hands quicker.

"N-no," I stumble over my words, trying to hold in my orgasm. "I-I'll choke you when I flare."

Nereus grips my hand, pulling it under the water to rub against his neck. Gills. Fuck, yes. Nereus has gills.

I relax again, my pleasure and the pressure building up some more. The tentacle in my ass pushes deeper, stretching me wide.

My hand squeezes Nereus' where we're still connected as the pressure finally explodes in me. The flares on my dick spread wide, locking me into place with him. He swallows down my cum, continuing to suck on me as he does. I get light headed from the sensations but his tentacles keep me upright as I go slack against them.

I can almost see his camouflaged head beneath the murky green water. Feeling satiated in a way that I haven't before.

It doesn't take long for my flares to go down. Nereus gently lets go of my cock, his tentacle easing out of my ass.

Chapter 18

Nereus

I wait under the water for a moment while Maddox catches his breath. I'm nervous about what his reaction to all this will be.

There's a pain in my chest from the need to have him accept me as his alpha. Maddox had said that he *wanted* me, but would that still be his reaction when I broke the surface?

I didn't really think that he wanted me at all. If I'm right, he just saw me as a means to an end last time.

My cock hangs heavy beneath my tentacles. I have a lot of steam that I would like to be blowing off myself right now. That's what convinces me to come back into the air.

Maddox has a satiated look on his face, but there's also a hint of concern. I need to be strong for him.

I bring our joined hands to my mouth and kiss his gently. To reassure him, but also to set my intent. This time it was not just a friend helping a friend. This time I had truly been shooting my shot.

Maddox shivers, hiding his face in my chest and nuzzling close to me. My arms wrap around him and I hold him close. His warmth seeps through me.

A hotter liquid hits my chest now, and I hear a little sniffle from Maddox. My chest burns with the realization that my mate is crying.

I shift us so that I am resting against the bank, Maddox curled up against my chest. I stroke his back soothingly.

"Did I push you too far?" I ask after a minute or two.

Maddox sniffles again, but he lifts his head to look at me properly. "No," he says, wiping at his eyes. "I think you finally pushed me enough."

His omega scent blossoms for me as he firmly places his hands on my chest. Maddox presses himself flush against me and I finally decide to bite the bullet.

"You smell like pine, amber, and chestnuts." I tell him, gently letting him know that I can smell his scent.

Maddox freezes against me.

"You can *smell me*, smell me?" He asks, his voice trembling.

I continue to stroke his back, nodding in confirmation.

"Ever since that audition in the back room of that dingy bar."

Maddox

Nereus is my mate.

He can smell my omega scent.

My mind wanders back to that first day when I met Nereus. Sebastian and I were looking for a drummer to record his first album.

God, Nereus had been such an asshole. When he had first walked into the room, I was immediately attracted to his 'fuck off' vibe and rockstar attitude.

I had hoped that he would be bad, just so that I could ask him out afterwards. But I knew that wouldn't be the case. Sebastian had sat up in his seat, clearly interested to see what a Kraken drummer would sound like.

Of course, Nereus had been amazing on the instrument. It was a bittersweet feeling, knowing that he would be in the band and that I wouldn't be able to date him.

But I hadn't wanted to be tied down to an alpha anyway, having the separation of the band would help with that. Or at least that's what I thought.

I spent years repressing my feelings for Nereus, despite all his flirty little comments.

"Are you telling me that when you walked into that audition room, you smelled your mate and you had *no reaction*?" I ask, incredulously, as the thought strikes me.

"Showbiz," Nereus chuckles. "My head was so big and my attitude was turned up all the way. I noticed, but I didn't *notice* right away."

I playfully smack Nereus' chest. "Six years and you didn't think to mention it?" My tone is playful, but there is a bit of bite in it.

Nereus flips us, my body shifting under the unexpected movement. I'm face down against the bank, my hands gripping at the slick mud for purchase. My dick is so hard already from that one move alone. I love it when he is rough with me like this.

"Do you really think you would've wanted me to?" Nereus growls in my ear, the sound sending a shiver straight to my hooves.

"Do you really think," Nereus reaches around me, gripping my dick hard. I can't help but buck against his hand. "That you would have welcomed your alpha with open arms?"

Two tentacles latch onto my shoulders from behind. Something hard and long presses against my back and I realize that it's his dick as Nereus grinds into me.

I whimper, a low omega whine. His cock feels different, there are some weird textures.

"I w—want to see," I say.

Nereus pulls back a bit, relaxing his grip on me so that I can turn around. He repositions his front tentacles on my shoulders again, so that I can see his dick.

"Holy fuck." It's huge, with a slight knot at the base. But that's not all, smaller tentacles are growing out from the base too.

Two more tentacles wrap around me, this time on my calves. They lift my legs up high, my thighs pressed as wide as they will go. We sink down into the water further at the shift.

"Are you going to take my cock, little omega?"

I whimper, nodding helplessly. I reach down to explore his dick with my hands. As soon as I touch him, Nereus growls, his head tipping back. "Fuck," he hisses.

My hands sink into the mass of tentacles as I cup his knot. Nereus uses my prone position to push a tentacle inside my ass, quickly spreading me wide and adding another.

I squirm against him, continuing to stroke his cock in my hand.

"Line it up," Nereus says as his tentacles pull out of my ass. I quickly press his head to my ass, doing as I am told.

Nereus thrusts into the hilt in one go, leaning forward and resting his head against mine. I whimper and writhe beneath him as he kisses me.

He grinds against me, keeping close as we both slowly work ourselves up. My pleasure builds to new heights.

"Tell me you're mine." Nereus says.

Tears pool in my eyes again as I reply, "I'm yours."

Nereus nods, groaning as he cums, his knot expanding inside me. "That's right, you're my little omega."

My release pools between us in the pond as I cum hard. It's not as much as last time, but I am spent.

Nereus gently turns us so that I can rest against him as I cry out at the overstimulation of it all. His knot pressing hard against my sensitive spot.

"Shh.. It's OK," Nereus soothes.

We lay there for a bit longer, keeping as still as possible as we wait for his knot to deflate.

We chat about the tour, and how it's going so far. How we're both glad that it's going to be a monster show tomorrow.

It feels so natural, laying there together in the water.

Chapter 19

Cleo

I twist in my sheets again, the banging noise and incoherent moaning just loud enough to keep me awake.

Flora stayed in our bus again tonight, but she brought Sebastian with her this time. I have no idea how she got him to fit in her bunk. Judging by the noises I'm currently hearing, he doesn't fit at all.

Sighing, I turn over again, trying to get comfy. Even if they weren't making a racket, I would still be struggling to sleep right now.

My thoughts keep straying to earlier today with Daisy. When she leaned into me, whispering about how hot she thought I was... I was glad when she bought me that lingerie, because I had most definitely soaked the panties right through.

Daisy's behavior was shocking, but even more so it was thrilling. It made me feel so sexy, her sitting in that chair as I tried on the clothes for her.

Afterwards, Daisy acted like nothing had happened. Well, maybe not completely normal. She touched me a lot more than usual, a hand on me at all times. Although, is that much different to normal? Or was I just more aware of it?

Either way, I can't help but replay all our little moments from the day in my mind. When I bucked my hip against her waist, feeling her hot breath on my neck as she whispered in my ear and made my toes curl.

Squeezing my legs together now, I try to relieve some of the ache that is forming in my core. I'm wearing one of my new sets, and it's oh so easy to flip up the tiny crop top to free my boobs. I cup one in my hand, teasing my nipple. The pleasure shoots straight to my clit, creating a throbbing sensation that doesn't help matters.

My other hand trails down my stomach, heading straight for my pussy to relieve the ache.

"I can't sleep," a whispered plea comes from outside my curtain. I have just enough time to pull down my top before Daisy is there.

"Those two are going at it like rabbits..." Daisy continues, not noticing that she almost caught me in a bit of a predicament. My heart is racing from the thrill of almost being caught.

"Yeah," I pant. "I can't sleep either."

Who was I to tell her that I had completely forgotten about the sounds coming from our friend's bunk. Daisy brushes some hair out of my face, and I have to force my breathing to be calm.

I've never been this nervous around anyone before, let alone Daisy of all people.

"How about we just go over to the guy's bus?" Daisy suggests, her hand lingering in my hair. "They're probably not fucking each other. So that's a plus."

She giggles at her own joke, so I join in awkwardly. Now I'm trying not to imagine what *that* would look like.

Maybe I'm ovulating or something, everything was just making me so horny at the moment.

"Oh God, you are sleepy, aren't you?" Daisy says, stroking my hair again. "Come on, I bet we can just share Sebastian's bunk and get a good night's sleep."

She holds out her hand and I take it, climbing out of my bunk in a daze. Share a bunk with Daisy? I really wasn't going to get any sleep tonight.

I head straight for the door on autopilot.

Daisy grabs my arm, pulling me to a stop. She tosses a sweater into my arms and puts my slides in front of my bare feet. Looking down at my tiny pajama set, my giggle is genuine.

We bundle up in our sweaters and quickly dash to the other bus, a short walk away. We jog to keep warm, but every few steps we devolve into a fit of giggles as at least one of our shoes slides right off.

"Cleo?" A deep voice calls. I turn to see Maddox running, gaining on us quickly. "Oh, and Daisy too? What are you doing out this late? You must be freezing!"

I gulp at the sight of the glorious minotaur. *Fuck.* Maddox was all sweaty, dressed in his workout gear, clearly out for a run.

"Flora has Sebastian over," Daisy answers. "They're being super loud and we can't sleep. So we were hoping that you guys might let us stay in Sebastian's bunk tonight?"

Maddox nods, keeping up with Daisy's words.

"Yeah, of course. Come on in." He heads towards the bus in question.

I breathe a sigh of relief, Maddox has been a bit strange with us recently, and I didn't know what his reaction would be. I start to move again, my legs burning from standing still in the frigid air.

"Let me make you both some tea," Maddox offers as we get inside. He passes us a blanket as we get comfortable on the couch.

Daisy gives me an amused glance as Maddox fumbles over the tea kettle in the tiny kitchenette.

"Mads, babe, is that you? Did you want to join me in the tub?" Nereus' booming voice fills the bus.

A crashing sound ensues as Maddox drops the tin of tea bags. Luckily, there isn't any damage or spills, but the noise clearly alarms Nereus, who comes quickly bounding into the space, shirtless.

"Umm... hi," Daisy awkwardly waves.

I stay silent, shrinking back a little and tucking myself against Daisy under the blanket.

Daisy hasn't seen Nereus since their kiss, and now he's calling Maddox *babe*? What the hell was going on?

"I dropped the tea tin, silly me. Do you want a cup?"

Maddox tries to pretend that nothing is amiss, but it's not convincing. Nereus nods to say yes to the tea.

"Good." Maddox continues. "The girls here have asked if they could stay over tonight. Their bus is currently occupied by some noisy tenants that they would rather not hear."

Nereus quickly recovers, "Yeah, of course. You can sleep in my bunk, I'll sleep in the tub tonight."

"OK," Daisy says with a little squeak. I place my hand on her thigh under the blanket to help calm her down.

"You know what?" Nereus continues, almost cheerfully. "This is a much better living arrangement. Flora and Sebastian clearly needed their own space anyway. It's about time that they just got their own bus!"

Maddox blinks at Nereus, a slight frown on his face that I can't figure out. This all seems a bit rushed, and Nereus was a little *too* positive about all this.

"I mean," I finally find the nerve to speak. "We can chat in the morning as a group and decide the best course of action."

Would that mean staying in a bunk with Daisy every night? Squinting down the hall, I look at the bunks again. They're pretty big honestly, much bigger than a human double bed.

Chapter 20

Daisy

Oh fuck. This is not going how I expected.

Living with the guys for the rest of the tour? It sure sounds like a lot. But then, so is having to listen to Flora and Sebastian every night. That's the alternative for either us or the guys if we don't come up with a solution.

The kettle sings, breaking us all from our thoughts. Maddox pours Cleo and I a cup of chamomile each, sliding them across the table to us.

"That should help you sleep." He says, gently. It is sweet that they are willing to take us in. I know I made out with Nereus, but Maddox doesn't have any reason to want to help us.

"Thanks Maddie," Cleo whispers, missing the absolutely adorable look on Maddox's face in response to her new nickname.

Nereus chuckles, sitting next to me while Maddox sinks down next to Cleo. A rogue tentacle caresses my ankle and I almost jump in surprise. Suppressing a shiver of pleasure at the contact, I look up at Nereus with a reassuring smile.

I don't think he had planned on me overhearing him call Maddox babe, but I've always noticed the sexual tension between the pair. I wasn't surprised that there might be something more between Nereus and Maddox.

My mind starts to wander about how they would work together, but I try to bring myself back to the present. Nereus continues to stroke my ankle under the table. He leans back, resting his arm on the back of the couch behind my shoulders.

Nereus thinks he is coy, gently toying with my curls. That is until Cleo calls him out. "Daisy doesn't like to have her hair touched. It makes it frizzy."

Maddox huffs out a laugh, his septum ring moving with the force of it. His horns accidentally scratch at the cupboard above his head with the movement. Cleo goes back to her chatting with Maddox, pretending like nothing happened.

Nereus leans his head down, speaking softly into my ear.

"What if we were in the water? Your hair can't get frizzy if it's already *wet*." He makes the word sound sinful. "Would you let me grab it then?"

Nereus wraps his tentacle tightly around my ankle as he speaks. My breath quickens, a lump forming in my throat as it dries up. Maddox's nostrils flare as he looks at me, almost like he's smelling me. I feel trapped, my chest tightening as I realize all of these beautiful people that I am between.

I nearly excuse myself when Cleo blurts, "Wow, this tea really is making me sleepy."

It snaps the three of us out of whatever stale mate we were in.

"I haven't had a sip yet," I admit. The tea really does warm me up instantly, contrasting with the cool kraken surrounding me.

"Are you looking forward to getting back on stage tomorrow night?" I ask Maddox, who is still staring at me.

"Yeah," he nods. "It's a pretty big deal in monster spaces, this venue."

"I'm sure you'll be happy to be back in a monster space."

Nereus replies this time. "It's not that we don't like the humans. They're just not fully receptive to us yet, so performing for them isn't as fun."

"I haven't really noticed a difference during our performances, if I'm being honest. But the house lights are always pretty dark for our set, and I can't hear much with our earpieces in anyway." I supply, taking another sip of my tea.

We chat for a little longer about our performances on tour so far, until our teas are long drained. Cleo starts to yawn and doze, as she usually does. But the three of us share a look and decide to keep chatting.

A few minutes later, Cleo snuggles into Maddox's giant arm, nuzzling against his warm fur. I hear when his breathing stops and he freezes, careful not to move.

Glancing up to Nereus, I wonder if he'll be jealous about it. But he's not, his eyes soften in a way that I haven't really seen yet. In a way that seems completely reserved for Cleo and Maddox cuddled together like that.

I can't blame him. Cleo looks so tiny, snuggled into the giant minotaur.

Maddox clears his throat, jostling Cleo and surprising both Nereus and I.

"Guess it's time we all head to bed." Maddox says.

Surprisingly, Nereus jumps into action, startling me in my own sleepy haze.

"I'll show you both to my bunk." Nereus holds out his hand to me, but I ignore it. I'm annoyed with his abruptness, at both of them. They jolted Cleo for no reason. I could tell that they both had thought she was being cute, so I didn't understand this change in demeanor.

I turn to Cleo, her sleepy eyes look hurt as she blinks up at me.

"Come on, baby." I clasp her hand. "Let's go to bed."

Cleo snuggles into my arm as we follow Nereus to his bunk. Luckily, it's the bottom one, so we easily climb in.

I snap the curtain shut in Nereus' face before he can say anything. Maybe I'm being dramatic, but I was sleepy. It had been a long night and I didn't take kindly to anyone putting out my little Cleo.

Lifting up the blanket, I help us both get tucked in. There's plenty of room in the bunk, but as soon as I lay down in the bunk properly, Cleo snuggles into me.

Chapter 21

Nereus

Maddox is still sitting in the same spot on the couch when I come back into the living space. He sits with his head in his hands, elbows resting on the table.

I felt bad for my mate. I could smell the exact moment his scent started to blossom, as he became more aroused when Cleo had cuddled into him.

Cleo's scent had responded in kind, a decadent and sweet vanilla. That's when it all made sense.

Crystal fucking clear.

"I really fucked that up," Maddox sighs.

"It's OK, we'll make it work. Let me help you out." I gently pat him on the shoulder.

I wonder if he is still rocking that insane boner he got for Cleo. Looking back, I could have handled it better, but I didn't want Maddox to be embarrassed. I hold out my hand to him now, his warmth enveloping me from that one touch.

My poor minotaur has had a long day. I take him to the tub room, locking the door behind us. I switch on the water and turn on some mood lighting before turning back to him.

Slowly and tenderly, I peel away his clothes, leaving gentle kisses on the newly freed fur on his chest. Maddox's cock is painfully hard, but I ignore it for now, gently maneuvering him into the tub.

We kiss, our bodies tangling together. I'm careful to make sure that we don't splash around or make too much noise. I gently turn Maddox away from me, kissing and nibbling on his neck. Moving his tail and my tentacles out of the way, I slide home, my cock filling him.

Fisting my hands in the mane of hair growing on the back of Maddox's neck, I shove his face down against the side of the tub. I've noticed that my minotaur likes it when I am rough with him.

My fucking is slow and deliberate, as I work out both of our frustrations. Maddox makes a low whining sound.

"Shut the fuck up." I spit in his face, rubbing it in. Maddox clenches around my cock hard, bucking back against me.

I grip his cock in my hand, fisting him under the water.

"Such a good boy, staying quiet for me."

We cum together, quickly spent after our day of fucking in the pond. My knot expands into Maddox and I move us so that he is resting against me.

"You did such a good job," I soothe, my knot still firmly pressed inside of him. "Taking my cock so well."

Maddox shivers against me and I give him a moment, stroking the fur along his chest.

"I have something to tell you." It's now or never, I can't keep withholding information from my mate.

"Something else you've been keeping from me?" Maddox pants through his words, his pleasure clearly building up again, my knot massaging him.

It's not lost on me that we only knotted for the first time earlier today. Poor Maddox isn't used to handling this level of constant pleasure. I continue stroking him gently, knowing that the juxtaposition between that and the hard pressure of my knot was probably driving him crazy.

"It's about us," I continue, pretending as though Maddox never made his snarky remark. "Us and the girls."

"They're our mates too, aren't they?" Maddox catches on.

I rest my chin on his head, nodding.

"I'm not sure how developed they are in their own relationship yet, if at all. And I didn't know it for sure, at least with Cleo, until I smelled her scent tonight. I realized with Daisy on the first day of tour, but I didn't want to push her. It's also why I didn't think there would be much of an issue with us both being into her. Also, why I wasn't too put off by you absolutely foaming at the mouth for her."

My chuckles hardly make any noise as I continue to place light kisses in the fur on the top of Maddox's head. He moans lowly as another wave of pleasure hits him. My minotaur cums again, panting quietly through it. I give him a moment before continuing with my thoughts.

"We need a plan to win them over. One where you don't keep scaring them off."

Chapter 22

Cleo

I wake up in a tangle of limbs, the scent of plums and cherries telling me that it's with Daisy. The proportions of the space throw me off for a minute. It's a bunk, but it doesn't have my usual art prints and ribbons lining the walls.

It takes me a minute to remember that we're in Nereus' bunk on the guy's bus. Last night almost feels like a blur.

Hmm... I guess this is mine and Daisy's space now. Maybe we will have time to move over our things properly today. Oh wait, we said we'd talk about it this morning. Daisy might not actually want to share the bunk with me.

It's weird, but I feel good about the idea of staying here with the guys. It feels right. And this is what tour is all about, being flexible and making changes when needed. It's all part of the fun.

Daisy shifts a little in her sleep, her thigh pressing forward in between my legs. I struggle to hold in a moan at the sensation. My eyes stray to Daisy's sleeping face, her pretty ginger lashes pressed flush against her cheeks. Laying next to the spattering of beige freckles on her pale skin. Her plush, full lips. I lick my own lips as I stare at Daisy's. Would it be softer than kissing a guy? Probably.

"Good morning," Daisy's groggy morning voice calls out. I was too distracted by her lips that I hadn't seen her pale green eyes open.

"Morning," I say. I can't help adding, "you look really pretty when you sleep."

Daisy's eyes widen a little at my confession, but she smiles. Her smile is a relief, I almost regretted the words as soon as they left my mouth. I decide to take a little action, a little risk.

"I keep thinking about the dressing room yesterday. How good it felt to have you take control like that. How *hot* it made me."

I run my hand up along Daisy's waist as I speak.

"Is that so?" She asks me, gripping my hips and pulling me closer. It sends a bolt of pleasure through me, my pussy pressed tight against Daisy's thigh. I whimper as I nod in confirmation.

"Can I kiss you?" Daisy asks, one of her hands moving up to cup my face.

I close the distance, not waiting to answer, just diving right in. Her lips are just as soft and plush as I imagined. We moan together at the contact, quickly pulling back, searching each other's eyes. I grin, showing her how good that felt.

Daisy tugs me back to her and I lose myself in her kisses. Grinding against her leg, I can feel my pleasure building. Daisy shifts us a little and she's grinding up on me now too. It's a lazy, sleepy rhythm that we set. Our kisses deepen, becoming more frenetic as we drive each other closer to the edge.

I can't concentrate on both at the same time, breaking our kiss.

"Oh, Daisy, I—" My pleasure flows through me. We pant hard as Daisy follows me over the edge. I tip my head back against the pillow, trying to catch my breath.

"Oh, *fuck*, Cleo..." Daisy sighs, gripping my hip hard. "We have been... Why haven't we..."

"I *know*." I answer. Why haven't we explored this before?

Chapter 23

Daisy

The curtain to the bunk hangs open as I wait for Cleo to be done in the bathroom.

A clicking noise sounds, and I notice some shuffling coming from the front of the bus. Leaning out of the bunk, I spot a glimpse of a white horn, a flash of a green tentacle.

"Morning," I call out. I quickly scrunch my curls, knowing that's all I can really do right now.

Getting out of the bunk., I have a clearer view of the guys. Maddox places a tray of coffee cups on the table, while Nereus clinks around in the cupboard, pulling out plates.

"Morning," Maddox calls back with an adorable little grin. "We brought you girls some breakfast to share."

He's so cute, but I also can't forget how weird he was last night and over the past week. Although, I can admit that I was being a little dramatic last night. We were all pretty tired and it was late.

Cleo comes out of the bathroom, peering around me to the guys.

"Ooh, is that breakfast?"

"Sure is," Nereus speaks.

I silently make my way into the bathroom and leave Cleo to deal with them.

Maddox

Life had taken a bit of a wild turn over the last 24 hours.

When I woke up yesterday morning, I was so annoyed with Nereus, and now he was my mate? I still can't believe how willing I was to accept that too, to accept him as my alpha.

Nereus had knotted me a few times now, and I felt so secure and safe and cared for with him. So far, I hadn't had any of the typical alpha issues that I would have expected. Had I been wrong to push back at this idea the whole time? I'm feeling a little insecure about the fact that I had been rejecting the concept of an alpha mate my whole adult life.

Then, on top of it all, these two beautiful human women were my mates too? I could never have expected to be so lucky. I want nothing more than to build a cozy nest for us all to hole up in for a few days.

But we are on tour, and tonight we were finally back at a monster venue. A great one at that. God, watching the girls tonight will hit different, knowing that they're my mates.

Heck, even playing on stage with Nereus will be completely different.

I still don't know how I feel about Nereus keeping this a secret from me all these years. But I do understand where he's coming from. From a timing perspective, this has worked out well. Especially now that we have the girls.

My weird unexplained horniness over the past week does make more sense now, anyway. I had been so obsessive, not being able to control my arousal around them, and it all made sense now.

It sucks that I needed to come across as a bit of an asshole in order to properly behave myself. I know I have some groveling to do to make it up to them. But Nereus and I made a plan last night. We were going to win the girls over.

Nereus had shared with me that Daisy was a bit pissed with him before bed, too. So we were both back at square one.

Step one of our plan was to get up early and wake the girls up with breakfast. But we had almost fucked up the timing with that when we came back to the bus and they were already awake.

Cleo wanders over to the table now, placing her tiny hand on my arm for balance as she slides into the bench.

"Here, we got your favorite." I tell her, passing her the lavender latte. Cleo pops the lid off, grabbing a stirrer.

"Ooh, it's so pretty!" she exclaims, stirring the foam to show off the purple liquid to me.

"Just like you," Nereus says with a wink, setting her plate of breakfast down in front of her. I almost think it's overkill, but Cleo blushes at Nereus.

Daisy grabs my attention, her eyes still sleepy, her curls wild. I didn't get to properly appreciate last night how cute she looks in that oversized sweater. She scoots in next to Cleo, her greedy eyes lighting up at the sight of the greasy bags on the table.

"Your breakfast is coming too, sweetheart." Nereus says as he preps Daisy's plate. I place a sweet caramel latte down in front of her with a grin.

"Thanks," she says a little timidly.

It's then that I realize the most work I need to put in is with Daisy. Whereas it's the opposite for Nereus, he needs to even start a relationship with Cleo. Nereus catches on too, as he gestures for me to sit next to Daisy.

I try to give her a friendly smile, but she seems a little off balance at that.

"Don't mind Daisy," Cleo says. "Her kindness is limited before she has her first sip of coffee."

"Drink up then," I tease, pushing her drink closer to her. She rolls her eyes, but I do get the slightest hint of a smile, and I consider that a win.

"Do you girls have plans today?" Nereus asks, sliding in next to Cleo.

Cleo starts to shake her head as the door to the bus busts open, Sebastian quickly filling the space in a panic. He opens his mouth to say something, but stops himself at the sight of the four of us having breakfast at the table.

"Fuck," he mutters, dashing back to the door. Sebastian calls out, "They're alright, Flora."

He comes back in, grumbling about how he thought the girls were missing.

"They very well could be," Nereus says, almost menacingly, standing up to full height. He gestures back to the door and Sebastian follows him outside for a word.

"Is Sebastian in trouble?" Cleo giggles.

"Nah," I say, although I'm not sure how much I truly mean it. "Nereus is pretty annoyed that you guys were wandering around on your own last night. He's probably putting some of the blame for that on Sebastian."

"We're grown adults," Daisy rolls her eyes.

"I'm *very* aware," I look her up and down to prove my point. Daisy nearly chokes on her coffee at my forwardness.

When Nereus comes back in, both Flora and Sebastian are with him. They all look a bit calmer.

"Sorry guys, we didn't think you'd be joining us." I pointedly look to the spread for four.

Sebastian shrugs. "That's alright, we can go get something ourselves. We just wanted to make sure that you girls were OK."

"Yeah, we were worried when we woke up and you were both gone." Flora fidgets with the bottom of her shirt. "Nereus was saying that you were thinking of staying here?"

"Maybe for a bit." Daisy replies, surprising me. "You and Sebastian should really have your own bus."

"Yeah," Cleo sighs, wistfully. "You're a mated couple, you need your own space."

My heart warms at the sight of Cleo like that, and I can't help the smile on my face. Soon, we will tell the girls all about it. But first, Nereus and I had a lot of work to do to earn their affection.

Chapter 24

Nereus

I couldn't help but give Sebastian a hard time over the girls being out on their own last night. But I regretted it when I saw the look of confusion on his face. I didn't want to have to answer questions about my feelings towards the girls either.

My behavior was already a bit overbearing and protective. I needed to cool it around the others for now. Otherwise, Sebastian will certainly figure things out before Maddox and I have had the chance to tell the girls ourselves.

At least my plan for us to all stay together was coming together nicely. I'm helping the girls move their things. Which basically consists of them packing up and me carrying.

I don't mind though, I'm happy to be able to help out my mates like this. It's also fun to see Daisy let out her bossy side, as she directs me around.

There's an interesting shift in Daisy and Cleo's behavior to one another too. They are a little more handsy, more so than just friends in general. But today, their touches are lingering, and Daisy is practically doing everything for Cleo. The true tell is those little smiles that they share, like they have a secret.

I can't help but think about how beautiful they would look in bed together. A clash of ginger and white blond. They really are both so stunning, especially in their graceful movements. It's obvious that they are both dancers.

Once they have their suitcases ready to go, I easily pick them up and walk us all to the bus. By the time we get there, Sebastian has already cleared his bunk.

Daisy and Cleo look at one another, an unspoken conversation going on that I'm not privy to. Shit, what if one of them wants to take Sebastian's bunk. They whisper now, too quietly for me to hear. Daisy's lips briefly brush against Cleo's ear as she says something that makes her giggle. Their decision made, they both start unpacking into my bunk.

I struggle to mask my sigh of relief, not entirely sure if I would have put my foot down at one of them not staying in my bunk.

"Are you sure you don't need a bed?" Cleo asks, mis-reading my sigh.

"I prefer to sleep in the water," I tell her, honestly.

She chews on her lip for a moment, deep in thought. But she reluctantly nods, climbing into the bunk and starting to decorate.

The bunks all have built in drawers at the foot of the beds, so I quickly empty the one in mine and move every-thing to Sebastian's. Then I leave them to their unpacking, knowing that I will most likely just get in the way.

Pulling open one of the slim closets in the living space, I take out my guitar and settle on the couch.

Playing drums is certainly my specialty, but I do like to play around on the guitar for fun. I look down at the faded stickers, the tiny scratches and dents on the woodwork. It brings back memories of Maddox and I messing around with it on our other tours.

It barely holds a tune anymore, and I get to work on it now. I couldn't bear to get a replacement though, the nostalgia worth all the tuning in the world.

We still had hours until we had to report in for sound check. Leaning back and getting as comfortable as I can, I start to gently play some of my favorite tunes to myself.

Playing guitar always helps me to calm down or think when I need it. Drums were for letting my feelings out in a cacophony, but the guitar was a soothing sort of release.

I wasn't a creative songwriter like Sebastian, I play lots of little melodies that I have learned over the years.

"Can I sit with you?" Cleo's voice gently asks.

"Of course," I start to put down the guitar.

"Oh no, you can keep playing." She says, "I'm just going to read."

She holds up an e-reader that's covered in pink, ballet themed stickers and ribbons. Her outfit is adorable too. Cleo wears leggings, with leg warmers over top, and a loose, thin sweater with a wide neckline hanging off one shoulder. Her skin is bare there, making it very clear that she's not wearing a bra.

Cleo curls up on the couch, looking so comfortable in the seat that is far too big for her. She pulls down a blanket from the shelf above her and snuggles underneath it.

I go back to my playing, keeping the sounds soft, my mind wandering as we sit together.

Chapter 25

Daisy

Cleo went out to read in the main space, and I'm happy for a bit of time to myself.

Last night was exhausting, and I think I'm processing too much on my sleep deprived brain right now. It's hard to get moments to yourself on tour, so I do try my best to get them when I can.

Maddox is out running again, apparently he goes out at least twice a day. I'm more than a little jealous of him. Going out for a run is something that I love to do. But with the lack of sleep, and a show tonight, I decided that it wouldn't be a smart move.

I had set an alarm to close my eyes for a bit, but my mind is reeling. The sounds of a soothing guitar playing in the faint distance was nice and relaxing though.

With everything else going on, I keep forgetting that I'm here to work. I have a job to do. My dancing is really important to me, and I take it very seriously.

There's enough space in the bunk to be able to sit up, so I start to do some stretching rather than nap. I've done much more complex shows on less energy than this before, so I'm not too worried about tonight.

I hear some rustling outside of my bunk. It's probably Cleo, and this is her space too. Sighing, I pull back the curtain.

Instead of Cleo's pretty face, I get a face full of Minotaur ass and tail as Maddox is bending over to reach into a bottom drawer. He stands up quickly, chuckling at my sassy curtain opening.

My jaw drops when he turns around, completely shirtless. Defined abs, pierced nipples, a chiseled 'v' leading into his shorts. My eyes wander back up to those pierced nipples, the hoops a perfect, smaller match for his septum ring. His fur is slick with sweat, having just come back from his run.

I can't help but thirst after how hot he looks. His soft, warm brown eyes crinkle at the edges as he realizes that I'm checking him out. He winks at me as he shakes out his clean t-shirt fresh from the drawer.

Neither of us say anything, but he keeps grinning at me as he walks to the bathroom and shuts the door behind him.

Running into a shirtless Maddox or Nereus might be happening more frequently, now that I was living with them. I can't say that I'm disappointed about that.

I might as well go into the main living area, at this point I'm not going to get much rest in my bunk anyway.

Cleo is curled up and snoozing when I come into the space, her e-reader resting unlocked next to her. Nereus is the one who has been playing the guitar that I heard from the bunk. The sunlight is filtering through the small window, showing off the lustrous glaze of his skin. He smiles at me when he sees me. I can't help but give him a little grin myself.

"Coffee?" I ask, softly, moving towards the little kitch-enette to make some. At his slight nod, I decide to make a full pot for us all.

Pouring two cups, I move to sit at the table. Nereus stops playing, joining me over there.

"Thanks," he says, settling in next to me. I get comfy on the bench, pulling my feet up and tucking my chin on my knees. Nereus turns to face me, resting his arm on the back of the bench and his chin on his fist. The muscles in his arm flex a little in the position.

"I didn't know that you played guitar," I say, taking a sip from my cup.

Nereus chuckles, "It's actually what I started playing first, and honestly still my favorite instrument."

"Wait, really? Why do you play the drums, then?"

"Because I'm really good at playing drums, and I'm only OK at playing guitar."

I just shrug at his response. His logic checks out, he *is* really good at playing the drums.

"I like watching you play," I admit. "After we're done our set, Cleo and I go up to whatever bar the venue has and watch you guys."

A rogue tentacle stretches up, stroking my thigh gently.

"Have you just been watching me? Or all the guys?"

I don't see any trace of jealousy on his face, his body language casual as he takes a sip of his coffee. He puts his cup down and places the hand on my knee, his thumb casually stroking me there. When I don't immediately answer, he continues.

"Because I want you to know that I don't mind. In fact, I would kind of like it if you were looking at someone else also."

I don't know what to think about that. I get being OK with me seeing someone else, but to actively want that? Maybe he is trying to tell me that he's poly? I had kind of picked up on that anyway.

With humans, being with more than one person at a time was kind of frowned upon. But I understood that it was different with monsters. It was pretty common with them, even. At least, that's what I had observed over the past almost year that I had been interacting with them. So I wasn't too surprised by all of this.

I think what surprises me is that *I'm* into it. I've clearly been looking at Maddox, and Cleo and I have developed things with each other.

Nereus and I had been flirting a lot over the past week, and our kiss was only a couple days ago. But I had also seen him be flirty with Maddox, and I was totally OK with that.

I think back to my kiss with Nereus, my pussy clenching as his tentacle wraps itself fully around my thigh, tightening. Nereus takes my coffee cup from my hand, setting it on the table next to his. He grabs my legs, pulling them flat over his lap and tugging me closer. He leans down, brushing his lips against mine.

"So…" he continues, "are you looking at anyone else?"

I find myself nodding as I lean back in for another gentle kiss. At that moment, Maddox walks into the room, grabbing my attention. He is rubbing his mane dry with a towel, his arm muscles flexing as he does, a strip of skin visible at his waist. I can't help but bite my lip at how sexy he makes that simple action. I realize my predicament, and try to pull away from Nereus' embrace.

"It's OK," he whispers to me, holding me in place. "We don't have to hide anything."

I find myself blushing hard, my cheeks feeling like they're on fire. I could just openly kiss Nereus in front of Maddox?

Shit. Cleo is in the room too. But when I glance that way she is still fast asleep, her mouth parted adorably.

"There's a pot of coffee." Nereus tells Maddox.

"Guess I better pour a cup for this little one, too." Maddox says, looking down at Cleo.

I try to pull away again, if Cleo wakes up and sees me like this, she might be hurt. Yes, she knew that I had something going on with Nereus. But should I really be shoving it in her face like this?

"So Cleo is someone you also look at..?" Nereus asks, noticing my panicked glance towards her. "You know, she might be more open than you think..."

Nereus relaxes his hold on me, but his words strike something in me. Cleo probably would be fine with this. But even more than that, I don't want to move away.

Instead, I grab my coffee again and curl up in his lap.

Chapter 26

Maddox

Knowing that Daisy and Nereus had kissed before, and seeing it in person, were two completely different things.

I am currently rocking a giant hard-on, breathing through my nose as I pour the coffee for Cleo and I. Taking the moment to myself, I readjust myself in my sweatpants to mask it as much as possible.

A few shaky breaths later and I can move back into the room. I set our cups down on the table and head over to Cleo.

"Hey, sweetie," I gently clasp her shoulder. "Let's get some coffee into you so you can do your job tonight."

Her bright blue eyes blink up at me as she nods her head sleepily. She pushes her hair out of her face as she sits up, and I want nothing more than to be able to scoop her up into my arms.

I squeeze into the spot next to Daisy, and Cleo slides in on my other side. I see the moment that Cleo registers that the other two are at the table. That Daisy is curled up in Nereus' lap. Daisy tenses a little, waiting for Cleo's reaction.

"That looks comfy," Cleo says, tucking her feet up and grabbing her coffee.

I sit upright, trying to give Cleo a comfortable amount of space on the bench, both of my hands in front of me on my cup.

"What were you reading?" Daisy asks Cleo, and they start to chat about a very unsettling thriller book.

I share a look with Nereus as the girls describe some of the gory details from the story. These women were clearly not scared easily.

The conversation develops into one that Nereus and I can contribute to, the show tonight. Cleo says how she feels really settled into the routine now, and that she feels like she could do it in her sleep at this point.

"That's good," I tease. "Because you fall asleep all the time anyway."

"Hey," she lightly smacks my arm.

The small bit of tension between us eases, and I put my arm around Cleo, resting it on the bench behind her. Cleo gets a little bit more handsy with me as we talk some more.

That's until Nereus announces that we should all grab a bite to eat with the crew before getting ready. We throw on our shoes and coats to head over to the catering tent.

Cleo sighs dramatically, claiming that she can't be bothered to walk there. To my shock, Nereus lowers himself pretty low to the ground, gesturing at his back and telling her to hop on. Part of me thinks that she won't, but Cleo happily climbs onto Nereus' back. She cackles with laughter as Nereus carries her all the way to the catering tent.

Daisy and I hang back, chatting a little, but more so just laughing at Cleo and Nereus. All of the crew members walking by stare at Nereus in shock, his usually stoic and grumpy demeanor nowhere in sight.

I'm so distracted by them that I almost miss Daisy tripping up a step. She grabs at me for support and I quickly catch her, holding her up.

"You OK?" I ask.

She continues to hold onto me, panic on her face and I'm wondering what I missed. She lifts up her foot in front of herself, testing the joint.

"Yeah, fuck." She sighs. "Thank you, that could have been bad."

Nodding, I realize now why she panicked. Daisy can't afford an injury like that mid tour.

I have to stay physically able for the tour, but I can't imagine the pressure that a dancer is under to keep their body perfect.

"You want me to carry you too, don't you? That's what this is." I joke, trying to lighten the mood.

Daisy looks at me for a moment, considering. "Nah, I'm good."

I'm not surprised about that one, Daisy doesn't seem like the type that wants to be held. Quite the opposite, I suspect. She does keep a hold on my arm though as we walk the rest of the way to the tent.

I make the effort to look after Daisy, picking up a tray for her and carrying her food as she plates it up. One glance shows me that Nereus is doing that for Cleo too, she blushes at whatever he's just said to her.

We join Flora and Sebastian at a table, and I catch Daisy watching Nereus and Cleo as they join us too.

"I'm surprised that they get along." She says to me.

"Nereus is an alpha," I explain to Daisy. "It's in his nature to protect. And Cleo is so innocent that I think he wants to protect that."

Daisy nods, picking at her food absentmindedly.

I leave her to her thoughts, wondering myself about how Daisy and I will eventually fit together. While I get along with her, and I'm obviously attracted to her, I still haven't quite figured out our dynamic.

Chapter 27

C*leo*

Daisy is radiant when we get off stage. Her curls have a halo of frizz, her eyes light up, and her smile is infectious.

I cling to her, doing our usual little happy dance. This time, the warmth of her body feels so much more inti-mate.

Nereus and Maddox watch us, but they're much more relaxed than usual. Maddox, especially. I still don't know why he had been acting so weird, but he seems to be back to normal now. His warm brown eyes light up with a smile as he catches me looking at him.

Nereus looks at us with hunger in his gaze. Well, I assume it's more so for Daisy than for me. He almost looks menacing in the dim lighting side stage.

"Good luck!" We call to them as Daisy and I move to go to the dressing room.

"Daisy," Nereus calls her back.

She goes back to him and he picks her up so that Daisy's legs wrap around his waist. Nereus kisses her, his hands tight on her ass. A pulse of awareness goes straight to my pussy at the sight.

Was I turned on by watching them? I look to Maddox, and he is gazing at them with just as much desire.

Daisy is blushing by the time Nereus sets her down. He whispers something in her ear that makes her blush even further.

I wonder if I should be jealous? But I've known that they have a thing going, and it hasn't made me jealous at all so far. Judging by the wetness pooling between my legs, I'm very much *not* jealous.

As Daisy walks back to join me, I realize that quite a few crew members just witnessed that. They're pretending that they didn't see, but I know that they will all be gossiping about it before we know it.

"Good luck," we call again before leaving to get changed.

When we get to the dressing room, Daisy rushes to get ready, as per our usual routine.

"Let's take our time tonight," I suggest, gently caressing Daisy's arm. "We can still make it out in time to see the guys."

Daisy blushes, so I continue on.

"Sorry, I just found you and Nereus kissing so fucking hot, and now I want some of the action too."

"Oh," Daisy seems to take a moment to get over the shock of me being so forward. But then she takes charge, and I relax into her embrace.

Daisy kisses me with more passion than she's shown me yet. The adrenaline from our performance mixes with the intensity of our kissing. I moan, feeling pleasure tingling through my body, I can't help but grind up on Daisy's leg.

"Wait." Daisy says. "Costumes off first."

I let out a little giggle, imagining having to explain those kinds of stains to the costume team. We both quickly slip off our body suits and before I know it, Daisy is standing before me in only her thong.

My throat dries out and I have to take a gulp, as I take in Daisy's almost naked form. Her tiny freckles and pale skin captivate me, I want to reach out and touch them. But Daisy's pale green eyes capture mine and all of a sudden she is lifting me up to sit on the vanity. She cups my boobs in her hands, toying with my nipples as she kisses me again. I slide forward, pressing against her for some friction.

"You really don't mind seeing me with Nereus?" Daisy asks, pulling away.

"Are you kidding?" I shake my head, incredulously. "I'm obsessed with it. You look so *good* together. Even at the table earlier when we were on the bus, I was entranced."

Daisy's lips are on mine again, but I could have kept going. I lose myself to our kiss, my hands roaming Daisy's soft skin. So different than being with any man, so soft and indulgent.

She kisses down my neck, her lips brushing the most delicious spot. Eventually, she makes it to my boobs, pulling my nipple into her mouth. Not for long though, because Daisy kneels before me. She pulls my panties to the side and her tongue dips into my folds.

A spark of pleasure hits me as her tongue finds my clit. It's so hard not to fist my hands in her hair. Instead, I lean back, my head resting against the mirror, as Daisy eats out my pussy.

It doesn't take long for my orgasm to hit me like a wave. I've never felt this good, my hands fisting at my boobs as I spasm with the pleasure.

Fuck, Daisy just gave me the best orgasm of my life.

Chapter 28

Daisy

Cleo leans against me on the love seat, her thigh pressed flush with mine. I'm hyper aware of every part of my body that's touching hers.

I keep a hand on her leg as we watch the guys perform. That is, until Flora joins us. I don't know why I felt the need to pull away a bit when she does. Cleo doesn't seem to mind, though.

The three of us chat on and off, but our main focus is on the stage and the guys there. I'm reminded of the conversation Nereus and I had earlier. How he had asked who I was looking at.

I'm pretty sure he has surmised by now that I have a thing for both Cleo and Maddox. Although, I don't know if Nereus knows that Cleo and I have acted on anything. I'm sure he knows that I haven't done anything with Maddox yet. Maddox would definitely share that with Nereus.

Heck, I barely even realized myself that I was *into* Maddox until earlier today.

I could almost be annoyed that all of my thoughts were being consumed by these three. But it was like Cleo had said earlier, I was familiar enough now with the set that I could probably afford to let myself take my focus off dance a little. As long as I was looking after my body, and Cleo's, I could let loose a little and get involved with multiple partners.

While I was happy with how things were progressing with Cleo, I did want to continue exploring things with Nereus further. Maybe even get to know Maddox a little better, too. Perhaps when they were done with the show tonight, we could have a private little party on the bus.

Flora is distracted at the bar, talking to some label rep. So I use the time to tell Cleo my plan.

"We haven't really talked about it too much, other than earlier. But you know that I'm into Nereus... well, I'm also kind of curious about Maddox." I tell her, my hand on her thigh again.

"M—me too." Cleo stumbles over her words nervously, and it's adorable. I want to lean in and kiss her so bad. "I really like Maddox. But I also kind of like Nereus too... is that OK?"

I nearly squeal with delight, squeezing Cleo's leg in my grip. Smoothing down her hair, I continue.

"It's more than OK. In fact, I'm really glad you said that... because I have a plan for our evening..."

Chapter 29

N*ereus*

I'm panting a little, sweat pouring down my back. It's always like this after playing a full set. Drumming is one of the only things that actually works out all my limbs at once.

It was the first time I had gotten to play with Maddox since I told him we were mates. His stolen glances back at me through our set warmed my heart.

I also spent a lot of the set wondering where the VIP bar was. I would need to ask at the next venue before we go on. That way I can at least feel like I'm performing for the girls.

I was still on a bit of a high from earlier when we went on stage. It was a mix between my kiss with Daisy, and the fun I had with Cleo earlier at dinner. Her lighthearted spirit lifted me up too. Cleo had helped me to feel more of a pure joy and I was grateful for that.

She was so beautiful, in such an innocent way. I was at war with myself, wanting to both protect and defile her.

Flora rushes past me and Maddox as we head backstage. Sebastian catches her up in one arm, handing his guitar off to a stage hand with his other. He spins her around and kisses her. Flora giggles and says something I can't hear, but it makes him grin.

Maddox has gone all gooey and soft, looking at them. It makes me happy to see him like that. Soon, we'll be able to share moments like that, with all of our mates. We just had to make sure that Maddox and I stayed firm in our plans to woo the girls.

For now though, I'm exhausted. I pat Maddox on the shoulder, suggesting that we go back to the bus for an early night. Maddox won't even need to go on a run tonight, the movement of the show enough to keep him sane. He should feel like he's gotten enough energy out of his system with that.

We meander back to the bus, my arm resting around Maddox's shoulder as we walk. I was surprised that Flora and Sebastian hadn't made a move to follow us, but I shrug it off.

Maddox enters the bus first, looking back at me in surprise. I follow him up to see that the lighting in the bus is dimmed and glowing. There is soft music playing, just loud enough to hear, but low enough to have a conversation over it.

Cleo sits in the center of the sofa, a cocktail in hand. She's wearing a tiny little dress that barely covers anything, especially with the way she is sitting.

Daisy is wearing a top and skirt that shows off a large strip of her midriff. Her skirt flows nicely over her ass, finishing just in time to cover it. She's at the kitchenette turned make shift bar, preparing cocktails.

"Hey guys," Daisy says. "I'm making margaritas."

"Is there a party you forgot to invite, well, *anyone* too?" I ask, closing the door and standing awkwardly by it.

"No, silly." Cleo says. "We thought we'd throw a house-warming, for the four of us. We even set Flora and Sebastian up with a little date in their own bus. So we'll be uninterrupted."

I can't help but wonder about how suggestive Cleo just made that sound. Surely not? The girls wouldn't have beaten us in the wooing department, would they?

No. I shouldn't read too much into it. They could genuinely just be trying to throw a little housewarming party. And I'm just being a creep.

I head to the bunk where I'm keeping my things, tossing my bag up there. Maddox follows close behind me.

"Are they..?" He starts to ask.

"I actually have no idea." I reply. "But we might as well go with the flow."

I take a moment to kiss my minotaur mate, partly in view of Cleo on the couch. I want to make sure that she can see us.

I subtly glance towards her, but she is openly staring our way, taking a sip from her drink.

Fuck. Maybe the girls are trying to proposition us?

Are they both trying to get with both of us? Or does each one have their eye set on only one of us? Does that mean Cleo would be going for Maddox? I had certainly laid a claim on Daisy earlier tonight when the girls came off stage.

Yeah, maybe that was it. Cleo was trying to get with Maddox.

I head over to Daisy with that in mind. But I see a quick flash of disappointment from Cleo that confuses me even more.

Leaning over Daisy from behind, I speak low.

"Those look good." She has quite the set up there, a cocktail making kit that I didn't even know we had on the bus.

"Thanks," she turns a little, smiling up at me. "I make them with frozen strawberries and basil."

Daisy picks up a strawberry, licking it suggestively, her tongue brushing her fingers.

"Want a taste?" She asks, feeding the strawberry to me before I answer. Then she licks her fingers clean. My cock grows heavy at the sight.

"Oops, you're making a mess." Daisy says, pulling my face lower and licking a stray drop of strawberry juice from my lips.

"Delicious." She comments, before turning and calmly continuing with her cocktail making.

"Cleo looks good tonight, doesn't she?" Daisy continues, not looking back to me as she speaks.

I'm not sure what I'm supposed to say. So I choke out a simple, "yeah."

"Why don't you and Maddox make sure she's *comfortable* while I finish up these drinks?" Daisy turns to look at me again with a smirk.

Fuck. I am so in over my head. These girls are playing us both tonight.

I take a moment to lock the door to the bus, making eye contact with Daisy as I do. Then I make my way over to the couch where Maddox is already chatting with Cleo.

Maddox has his arm up on the back of the sofa, and Cleo is turned to face him. Her body language is giving off major vibes that she's into Maddox.

"Nereus," Cleo says cheerfully. "Come join us."

She pats the spot next to her and shifts so that she isn't leaning as much towards Maddox anymore. The move makes her skirt ride up a little, the top of her dress pulling down at the same time to dip further between her boobs.

I can scent all of my mates around me, vanilla, chestnuts, plums. Their scents tell me how turned on they all are, and it's so intoxicating.

Mirroring Maddox's body language, I put my arm over the back of the couch too. My hand strokes Maddox's arm and I leave just enough space between us that one shift from Cleo would have us touching.

"That looks tasty." I say, pointedly looking at Cleo and not the drink in her hand.

"Would you like to try some?" she asks, blinking innocently up at me.

At that moment, Daisy brings me a drink of my own. I cheers with Cleo, clinking our glasses together before taking a sip. It's delicious.

Daisy comes back again with two more glasses. There's space next to me, but she passes one to Maddox and sidles up next to him on the couch. Maddox twists a little so that he doesn't have his back to her.

He looks surprised that she chose to sit next to him. But I get less and less surprised as the evening goes on. Daisy positions herself on her knees for some added height, and rests her arm up on the back of the couch. She's very much asserting her dominance over Maddox with that position, and it's sexy as fuck.

"Cheers," Daisy says, her skirt flowing perfectly around her as she holds up her drink. "To new roommates, and to new *experiences*."

Oh boy. I was fucked and I could not wait. I watch as Daisy strokes a hand down Maddox's mane, "what do you think?" she asks.

I don't catch his answer though, distracted by Cleo next to me. She was tall for a human woman, but she looked slim and fragile between Maddox and me.

"Do you like it?" she asks me. "It's Daisy's specialty."

Nodding, I agree that it's good. I try out something, bringing a tentacle up to brush against Cleo's knee.

"Ooh," she lets out a breathy sound. "I wondered what those would feel like."

I indulge her, explaining the different textures and feelings I could create with them. Showing her on her skin as I go. This was turning her on. If the little blush across her cheeks wasn't signal enough, the shifting sweetness of her vanilla scent was. I'm glad that she was finding it attractive, I had been nervous that Cleo wouldn't be into my tentacles.

"Daisy told me that you had an interesting tongue too..." Cleo continues. I'm certain now that the girls mean to seduce us. So I decide to tease her a bit.

Taking a sip from my drink, I nod in agreement.

"I suppose you could call it interesting."

Cleo doesn't back down though, which is exciting. "Do you think you could show me?" She asks, stretching up a little more.

Does she want me to kiss her? I'm pretty sure I know what's going on here, but I don't want to overstep, either.

"Do you want to see it?" I lean closer, locking eyes with her piercing blue. "Or do you want to *feel* it?"

Cleo nods gently. "Feel it," she says with a breathy sound, raising up onto her knees.

I catch the back of Cleo's head in my hand, my deep green skin standing out against her white blond hair. I press my lips against hers once, testing her out. She doesn't pull away, so I move in again, pressing my tongue into her mouth to explore her.

Cleo moans in response, her hand coming up to press against my chest. Kissing Cleo is so similar and yet so different to kissing Daisy. They both have that softness of human women, but where Daisy rises to meet my challenge, Cleo becomes pliant and submissive beneath me.

I love both equally.

Chapter 30

Maddox

Daisy has been handsy with me since taking her seat. I'm so aroused by her leaning over me, that I take a gulp out of my margarita to help calm my nerves.

"It's a drink for sipping, you know." She teases, gently smoothing out some of the hair in my mane.

"You don't mind me touching you, do you?" She paus-es, and I immediately shake my head to have her touching me again. "Good, because this hair definitely got ruffled on stage."

She continues to smooth out my mane and it's so hard not to practically purr. I can't help but be turned on as she grooms me, especially in that outfit. Daisy has raised herself up, leaning against a cushion so that she is closer to my height.

"You played really well tonight." She says. "I was watching you."

Daisy takes a sip of her drink, flashing her green eyes at me.

"You were?" I gulp. I wasn't surprised that the girls watched our set. But the thought of her watching me play, and then wanting to lean over me like this...

"Yeah, we always go to the bar and watch you both play."

I'm completely entranced by Daisy as she continues to stroke me. I would do anything she asked of me right now.

Her stroking of my fur slowly moves up to my jawline and cheek.

"You're so smooth here. It's like velvet," she continues her exploration. "I liked your piercings when I saw them earlier." She says, glancing to my chest.

My shirt covers the piercings, but I flush anyway, knowing that she knows they're there.

"Would you look at that?" Daisy says, her lips turning up into a smirk. I follow her gaze to find Cleo practically in Nereus' lap, kissing him. Nereus pulls back, making eye contact with me, a smirk on his face.

Nereus says something to Cleo, but I can't hear through the blood rushing from my head straight to my dick.

Cleo and Nereus fall back into conversation as they finish their drinks. I look back to Daisy to see that she's watching me, biting on her lip. She glances down to my crotch and raises an eyebrow at me. I just know that my dick is bursting at the seams of my jeans. I blush, knowing that Daisy knows why.

"If you finish your drink, I might help you with that." Is all she says, taking the last sip of her own cocktail. She chuckles as I down the last of mine, taking my glass from me, leaning across the space to place them on a side table.

The move makes the globe of Daisy's ass nearly entirely visible and I huff a desperate groan, struggling to keep my hands to myself.

When she turns back with a grin, I realize that she did that on purpose. Was she really going to help me with this hard-on? Was she really making a move with me?

She settles back into her spot next to me, her hands moving to cup my muzzle. I tentatively place my hands on her waist. She feels soft and warm beneath me, and I can't help but knead her there.

Daisy leans forward, and while she has been all confidence up until now, she falters a little regarding my mouth. I let her keep control though, letting her press her lips gently to mine.

She feels so delicate against me, her tongue gently teasing into my mouth. I caress her back, but I let us stay firmly in my mouth as she grows in confidence and moves more aggressively against me.

Daisy reaches between us, and her small hand presses against my dick. I can't help the needy little whine that escapes me at her touch. She presses hard, her hand creating a warm friction against the denim that drives me wild. She pulls away from our kiss, still stroking me hard.

"Do you like that?" There's a teasing tone in her voice that says she knows very well how much I'm enjoying her touch.

"Good boy." My mind empties out into pleasure at her praise.

The sensations of Daisy stroking my mane again with one hand and my dick with the other starts to drive me into a frenzy.

Chapter 31

Cleo

I continue to chat with Nereus, now that the tension has calmed down. But I can't get over how good that kiss felt. His tongue was rough and made me feel things I didn't know were possible.

We sit touching now, his cool skin pressed against mine. I almost lean in again, but a low, whining sound gets my attention in almost a primal way. Turning, I see that it came from Maddox.

Daisy straddles his lap, her hand reached between them and pressing on his cock, I would assume. They're kissing, and Maddox is bucking up against her. Daisy's full ass is on display, her skirt caught up in Maddox's fists.

Nereus pulls me back against him, so that I'm sitting in his cool lap again.

"They look so good together, don't they?" He says, stroking my hair back. It bares my chest to him, giving him an eye full. I can't help but agree with him. Daisy is clearly taking charge, using her body to control Maddox.

Watching Maddox come undone with another whining sound sends a wave of pleasure through me. My breaths become more shallow, and I'm keenly aware of Nereus' hands on my waist. He holds me close as we watch.

Nereus raises a hand, his knuckles brushing against my nipple through the thin fabric of my dress. I cry out at the unexpected touch, surprised with the intensity of the sensation.

Daisy and Maddox turn to look at us. Nereus, ever the showman, purposefully strokes and pinches my nipple through the fabric. I can feel more pleasure blooming at my core. Daisy makes eye contact with me, and we share a knowing smile. This evening is going perfectly to plan.

Maddox lets out another low whine and there's something about that sound that speaks to my soul. Nereus' hand dips lower, teasing at the hem of my dress, which is barely covering anything at this point. He lifts it up to my waist, while his other hand pulls down the neckline, exposing my boob to the cold air. He cups me, his cool hand making my nipple harden almost painfully. Nereus gently maneuvers me, lifting my leg up to bend at the knee, setting my foot flat on the couch so that my legs are spread for him.

"That's it, princess. Show me your pretty pussy." I clench at his words. Nereus reaches his hand down to cup me there. I moan at the contact, pushing my hips forward to create friction against him.

I reach down and stroke one of Nereus' tentacles, enjoying the slick feel of them beneath me. I'm hot from my arousal, but the coolness of Nereus feels amazing. I know that Nereus must be able to feel how wet my pussy is through the fabric of my panties. But instead of being embarrassed, I'm turned on even more by the thought.

"Are you going to be good for me, princess?" Nereus asks.

I'm not even really sure what he means, but I nod anyway. I would be whatever he wanted right now.

"Good." He strokes my nipple again, earning another moan from me. "Because I want you to take my tentacles."

Excitement flows through me at the thought and I bite my lip. This is something I have been dying to try with Nereus.

"Yes, *please*." I say, writhing on his lap.

His tentacles come at me all at once, and despite my enthusiasm, I do become a little nervous.

"Just relax for me, princess."

I do. His words wash over me and I relax into submission for him. I feel safe with him.

A tentacle wraps around my neck creating a gentle pressure, the tip pressing at my lips. I open to it, wrapping my tongue around the tip, gently suckling. It feels a lot thicker than I expected. Another one has wrapped around my ankle on the couch to hold me in place, while yet another wraps around my other leg, spreading me wide for him. He leaves my arms unbound, and I cling to him

"Pinch my arm if you want me to stop."

Nereus doesn't wait much longer. The hand on my pussy grips the fabric there, moving it to the side. A tentacle winds its way up my body. Nereus cups my boob in his hand so that the sucker on his tentacle can latch onto my nipple. I cry out at the sensation of it pulling and sucking on me. The sound that leaves me next is a desperate whine, which gains me the full attention of Maddox and Daisy. I had almost forgotten that they were there for a minute, completely distracted by Nereus and all of his limbs.

The suction on my nipple was more intense than I had imagined when dreaming about what it would be like to get with Nereus. My bare pussy writhes against nothing, another pained whine escaping me.

Daisy blinks at me, her focus returning, realizing that she has her own pleasure to take.

"Take off your shirt," I hear Daisy say to Maddox, who quickly obliges. Daisy flicks her hair, smirking at me, and I understand that she was providing me with some delectable eye candy. Maddox shirtless is incredible, all chiseled muscles and pierced nipples.

A tentacle probes at my pussy. I was so distracted by Maddox that I didn't see it coming.

"Oh, fuck." I cry out as the tentacle eases in and out of me, the sound muffled by the one in my mouth. Nereus' fingers work my clit, and I grip his arms hard. I move my hips against him, taking him deeper.

Losing myself to my lust, my hooded gaze shows me Daisy straddling Maddox, his nipple between her teeth. She grinds down on his cock to the beat of the music playing in a sensual dance.

I cum with a gush of liquid, the orgasm coming upon me from nowhere. I realize that I've squirted all over Nereus.

"Oh, shit," I start. "I'm so sorry, let me—" I try to move to clean him up, but Nereus holds me in place.

"Stop." He says it in such a commanding tone that I relax like putty against him. "That was fucking beautiful."

Relaxing against him more, I let myself enjoy the afterglow of the orgasm, his tentacle still resting inside me.

"Maddox," Nereus says, pulling his attention away from Daisy. "Cleo here has made a bit of a mess of herself. Be a good boy and come clean it up."

Daisy chuckles as Maddox looks torn, his glances straying between Daisy and us.

"Well, you heard him." Daisy says, climbing off of Maddox's lap.

Maddox quickly moves to us, coming to his knees before me. He starts to lick my juices off Nereus' tentacles. I'm surprised by how erotic the image is, Maddox's horns grazing against my foot.

Daisy strides over, standing next to Nereus. I assume that she is going to touch me, but instead, she leans forward and kisses Nereus. It puts her boobs right in my face. I take the opportunity, pulling up her top to expose them to me.

Daisy pulls away, chuckling, but it's to pull her top off altogether. She leans back in to make out with Nereus, and this time I grab her boobs in both hands. Nereus pulls his tentacle out of my mouth, and I quickly replace it with Daisy's nipple. The tentacle that was wrapped around my leg has moved to Daisy, but the one inside my pussy starts to thrust again.

I moan around Daisy's boob, my pleasure starting to build again. Instead of rubbing my clit, Nereus' hand moves to free my other boob. He massages and pinches at my nipple, his tentacle sill sucking on my other one. The onslaught of sensation is almost too much.

Something wet and warm engulfs my pussy and I cry out. A glance down shows Maddox has moved his cleaning right to the source. He laps at my clit while the tentacle continues to fuck me. I grip his horns in my hand and grind against him. The noises he makes as he tastes me are sending me over, all of the competing sensations driving me crazy.

The tentacle around my neck constricts and I free Daisy's nipple with a gasp. I orgasm again with a loud cry, Maddox licking up all my juices.

Daisy and Nereus break their kiss, both watching me intently with hungry gazes. All I can manage is to smile up at them in a daze.

Maddox rises before me, pulling me into his arms, the tentacles around me falling away easily. I snuggle into his warm chest. My overly sensitive nipples brush against his fur, making me whimper.

Nereus and Daisy stand up to join us. Nereus bends down and drags me under with a deep kiss, his tongue exploring me.

Chapter 32

Daisy

"I made sure that the tub was hooked up and ready to go if we needed it." I tell Nereus as he pulls away from Cleo.

"Also," I turn to the group. "It turns out that Nereus has been hogging a whole hot tub, with *jets*." I tease, Cleo gasping from Maddox's arms.

"There's *jets*?!" she squeals, showing me that there is a lot of life left in her yet. Even after both of those incredibly sexy orgasms.

"Oh, yeah. I kind of forgot about those." Nereus says, rubbing the back of his head.

"You can make it up to me," I say, running my hand up his shirt, feeling his torso for the first time. Nereus feels as smooth here as he does everywhere else, but a muscular smoothness.

He takes off his shirt, tossing it to the floor and exposing all that delicious green skin to me. I lick at his chest, as his hands reach around me to unzip my skirt, pulling it down over my hips.

I stand before him in only my thong. Nereus steps away, drinking in the sight of me. It's both nerve wracking and empowering at the same time.

"You are so fucking sexy." Nereus leans down and runs his tongue along my nipple. The rough texture feels amazing there.

"Turn around for me. I want to see your cute little ass." I turn around, bending forward and resting my arms on the table. I arch my back, my legs spread slightly, giving him a full view.

One of Nereus' tentacles lashes out, trapping my arms in place. I cry out in shock, looking to the others, but they're not in the room anymore.

"They went to the tub," Nereus explains. "You're all mine."

I whimper with anticipation as Nereus slides my panties down my legs. I cry out again when a hand smacks against my ass, the sting shooting straight to my clit.

"You have such a good ass," he tells me, squeezing it. "You're being such a good girl for me, too."

He smacks me a few more times, each one felt in my clit. Then he dips his hand between my legs from behind, feeling the wetness pooled there and spreading it around before letting me go.

When I turn back to face him, Nereus is licking his fingers clean, his stormy eyes fixed on me. I moan at the sight, pulling him down to kiss me so that I can taste myself on him.

"Tub's full!" Maddox calls from the back of the bus.

I pull away, Nereus smacking me on the ass again as we head to the tub room.

The space is filled with steam, and Cleo is on her knees before a completely naked Maddox, his cock in her mouth. Cleo looks beautiful, but I can't help but be distracted by

Maddox's cock. I kneel down next to Cleo to get a closer look.

His shaft is large, with a bump around the middle. The end has a series of ridges that move in rhythm as Cleo sucks on his head. Leaning forward, I tease some of the ridges with my tongue, and they flare outwards under my touch.

After a minute, I decide I want a moment with Cleo to check in. Pulling her away, I wrap my arms around her, kissing her deeply. It's nice to have a moment alone.

Cleo pulls away from me, panting gently, her face flushed.

"Wow, three orgasms in one night?!" I comment, loud enough for the guys to hear, hinting at the fact that Cleo and I were busy earlier tonight. I tickle Cleo, eliciting a cute little giggle.

"Wait, *three*?" Nereus pulls me back by my hair to look at him. I just wink, earning some more giggles from Cleo. Nereus lets out a surprised laugh, letting me go and climbing into the tub.

Maddox joins him, climbing over the edge. I'm fascinated by this tail, the little tuft of fur at the base. Cleo and I are still kneeling on the floor together, out of view.

"You doing OK?" I check in. Cleo vigorously nods, a huge grin on her face.

"How could I not be?"

That's a good point. The guys have been incredible so far, and our plan has worked better than I expected.

We stand up, Cleo still wearing her dress. She faces the tub, so I stand behind her, baring her to the males as they watch from the water. I kiss Cleo's neck and shoulder as I free her from the garment.

Once I have her free, I realize our predicament. Even standing on the step, we're too short to get into the tub on our own.

Nereus moves out of the tub a bit, his slick tentacles gripping the sides. He lifts Cleo in first, then me. Cleo makes a straight beeline for Maddox, curling up against him in the warm water.

Nereus keeps a hold on me as he eases me into the water. He gives me a slow and sensual kiss as we get comfortable. He's left me wanting too long, his kiss too slow. I grind up against his torso, but he's too slippery against me and I can't create any good friction.

I can't help myself, curiosity and maybe a little bratti-ness taking over.

"You do *have* a dick?" I lean back and ask.

Maddox cracks up laughing behind me, the space is so small that I can almost feel him there. Cleo moves to Nereus' side, as Maddox presses himself and his cock into my back. I wiggle back against him, my head tipping back to rest on his chest.

"I don't mind if you don't have a dick," Cleo says, stroking Nereus' cheek adorably. "Your tentacles are *more* than enough."

Maddox busts into another fit of laughter, and I can't help my smile. He wouldn't be laughing so hard if Nereus didn't have a cock.

"I have a dick, ladies." Nereus shoots daggers at Maddox, but his heart isn't really in it. "Although, I also have a *very* unruly minotaur."

Maddox sobers behind me, and all of a sudden I feel like I'm being used as a shield. Maddox pulls us back against his side of the tub, creating a little space between us and the others.

The smile that Nereus wears is all predator, and even I'm a little nervous. He stalks to us, his tentacles stretching to fill the full space, lifting his torso out of the water. Both Cleo and I are trapped in our positions.

"Daisy," Nereus says, and I feel the full attention of the predator in the water. "What do you think we should do to him?"

Oh, this is fun.

I move closer to Nereus, and he shifts his tentacles to let me get close to him. Taking a bit of a risk, I reach forward under the water, fumbling until my hands meet a cock as big as Maddox's. I stroke him for a moment, watching his eyelids droop a little with the pleasure, his breath becoming uneven.

"Maybe you should fuck his mouth with this," I suggest.

"Great idea." I can only describe Nereus' smile as wolfish in that moment.

I find myself being gently shifted by his tentacles to sit next to Cleo. We climb up so that we sit on the ledge, leaning back against the tiled wall. I pull Cleo against me so we can watch.

Nereus wraps his tentacles on the free edge of the tub around Maddox, his other appendages pull him further into the water so that his head is level with Nereus' cock. I had felt it, of course, but seeing it was an entirely different thing.

It was a darker color than the rest of Nereus, and I realize now that I had only felt the tip. I had completely missed out on all of the smaller tentacles growing out of the base of Nereus' cock. I also missed out on the giant knot at his base.

Nereus' shows no mercy, spitting in Maddox's face before he shoves his cock down his throat. I would almost feel sorry for Maddox, but from the sounds he is making, I can tell that he's enjoying himself. Nereus fucks Maddox's mouth with a force that I don't think Cleo or I would be able to take. I can see why he would need a partner like that.

The entire scene is incredibly erotic, and I start to play with my nipples as I watch. While it's been so good to watch everyone else get a piece of the action tonight, I am a horny mess. I need release.

Cleo senses my dismay, she reaches between us, rubbing my clit. Her touch sets me alight, stoking the flames of my already fiery arousal. She stops her movement, and I almost drag her hand back, but she plops into the water before I can.

Settling herself between my legs, her tongue delves into my pussy. "Fuck," I sigh as she alternates between that and licking my clit with precise movements.

Nereus pulls his cock from Maddox's mouth, telling him to keep his mouth open. He spits into his mouth before smacking him across the cheek. Maddox clearly gets off on the degradation of it all, and I wonder what it would be like to degrade him like that myself.

Cleo continues licking at my clit, and it sends me right over the edge. I watch Nereus pull Maddox in for a deep kiss at the same time. The whole scene, with Cleo too, is what does it for me.

The guys pull away to watch when they hear me cumming. Nereus comes up behind Cleo, encouraging her to keep eating me out through my orgasm. My pleasure builds even further, my eyes shutting as I let go to it.

Something slippery touches off my leg, and before I know what's really happening, a tentacle is pushing up into me. It presses against my g-spot, massaging, as Cleo continues to lick my clit.

It doesn't take long for another orgasm to crest through me.

Chapter 33

Cleo

I flick my tongue against Daisy's clit as Nereus' tentacle moves in her. She's making the sexiest noises, her hips bucking against us. Daisy just came, but Nereus instructed me to keep licking her through it again.

Nereus' hands reach around me, moving to play with my nipples. The slippery feel of him in the water is a completely different sensation to earlier. One of his tentacles finds my pussy, and before I know it I'm being fucked again. Except this time, Nereus is pushing up further into me.

"I need to stretch you out so you can take my cock," he tells me. Both Daisy and I moan when he says that.

I glance up and see that Maddox has joined Daisy on the ledge. She strokes his cock as they make out. Nereus steals my attention again, pausing in his thrusting. Instead, one of his suckers has started to suck right on my g-spot. I have to abandon Daisy's pussy. It feels so good, my mind turning to mush at the sensation. I would sink to the bottom of the water if Nereus wasn't holding me up.

He leans down and kisses me through the best orgasm of my life. I cling to him, my body spent. Nereus won't give me rest though, he starts to fuck me with his tentacle again, thrusting deep inside me. Now that I have cum like that, I feel the walls of my pussy relax around him as he stretches me wide.

Nereus moves me away from the others, pulling us back toward the front of the tub. I'm barely coherent enough to see that Maddox and Daisy are entwined in one another, his fingers deep in her pussy.

I like that I have Nereus all to myself. Looking up at him, he pushes my wet hair out of my face as he continues to fuck me hard with his tentacle.

"You're doing so well for me, princess." He says, easing his pace. I can't help but clench around him.

"I want your cock," I whine.

To my joy, Nereus nods. "We can try, but you have to tell me if it's too much OK?"

"Yes, daddy." The words fall out of my mouth. I haven't ever called anyone that before.

"I like that," he says, pulling me in for another kiss.

He presses me against the wall of the tub. His front tentacles brush against me as he moves them to either side. I reach between us to stroke the head of his cock, guiding him to me.

Nereus stares into my eyes as he slowly eases into my pussy. I feel myself stretching wide around him, there's a brief burning sensation before I'm filled with ecstasy. He keeps pushing until I can feel his knot pressed against me, his smaller tentacles tickling me.

"Fuck." Nereus pants, leaning over me. "You're so tight, princess."

I'm beyond coherent speech. I let out breathy moans and sighs as we come together. His little tentacles press and wriggle against my clit as he fucks me slowly.

Nereus continues to tell me how good I'm doing, how well I'm taking him. I can almost hear him, but I'm completely lost to the pleasure.

He pushes in that last way, finally. His knot stretches me even wider as he cums inside me. I can't help the flurry of orgasms that shoot right through me.

Nereus turns us so that I am laying on his chest. My head flops down onto him, my energy spent. He strokes my back through my orgasms, his knot still pressed hard against my clit.

Maddox

My fingers are stuffed deep in Daisy's pussy, the warm tightness making my cock even harder in her hands. We sit on the ledge of the tub, my tongue deep inside her mouth as we kiss.

Daisy writhes against my hand, and I'm worried she's going to hurt herself on the tile.

"Come here," I say, pulling her down into the water with me. I sit, pulling her onto my lap, and my fingers find her pussy again. I massage against her sensitive spot and she eventually unravels around me.

She rests her head on my chest for a moment to catch her breath. But she recovers quickly, reaching between us and lining my cock up with her pussy.

"Wait," I pant, and Daisy freezes in her movement "I just want you to know that I'm going to cum a *lot*. It's a minotaur thing and my dick will lock us in together and my cum will fill you up."

I rest my hand on her stomach to emphasize my point. Daisy kisses me deeply, her tongue exploring my mouth. She reaches between us again and guides my dick into her pussy. She sinks down a few inches, her gasp breaking our kiss.

"That sounds fucking *amazing*." Daisy exclaims.

She grips my throat with one hand, her other toying with my nipple piercing. Fuck, the warm grip of her pussy, the pinch on my nipple, her hand on my throat, it's all too much. I want her to choke me, to boss me around.

Gripping her by the hips, I keep her steady as I thrust up into her, getting deeper with every thrust. It's not a power move by any means, I'm trying to take the load of the physical exertion for her so that she can enjoy herself.

She cries out when I get a little bit deeper. I can't get over how tight she is, squeezing around me. I pause us for a moment when we get to my medial ring, to give her a break. Daisy pushes herself over it, moaning at the sensation. It sends her into an orgasm and I can't breathe through her clenching of my dick. She squeezes my throat hard with both hands as she cums.

I barely hold out, struggling not to cum when she allows me to breathe again. Daisy takes a break, thankfully. She rests her head against my chest, panting heavily.

Stroking Daisy's hair, I look over to the others. Nereus has a content Cleo resting against him, knotted to his dick. They're watching us, I realize. I can't help but buck against Daisy with how turned on that makes me. To know they are watching us like this.

Daisy gathers her strength and meets me thrust for thrust. She continues to grip my neck with both hands as she pushes and grinds against me.

My orgasm blows through me, my release forcing its way into Daisy's pussy, my flares locking us tight together. She screams at the feeling of my flares, pushing against her walls and her g-spot.

I continue to buck against her, filling her with my cum for a solid minute. Daisy cries out with orgasm after orgasm, tears streaming down her face from the pleasure of it all.

Her slim form shows the mound of her stomach as I fill her up with my cum. Fuck, that is the most beautiful sight. I place a hand on her stomach before pulling her in to kiss me. We writhe against one another as she keeps expanding, until I am finally spent.

"Fuuuuuck," Daisy cries out, tears streaking her cheeks.

She kisses me again, and I'm overcome with how good she feels. How perfect this moment is. I want to fill my mate up with cum every night.

Daisy wipes away my own tears, sharing this vulnerable moment with me. We patiently wait through the onslaught of sensations.

Luckily, my flares go down quicker than an alpha knot. Once they are down, I gently ease out of her.

I lift Daisy up onto the ledge of the bath again so I can watch as my cum slowly leaks out of her.

"I wanna see," Cleo pipes up from behind me. I move aside so that they can see her a bit better. Rubbing my finger against Daisy's clit makes her cum again, and it helps more of my cum to leak from her.

Daisy's stomach is flat now, but all I can think about it getting to fill her up again.

She looks so beautiful, spent and mussed up for me.

Pulling her back into my arms, I wade back to the others.

Chapter 35

Nereus

Maddox carries Daisy over to Cleo and I. She's in a satiated daze, quite like Cleo still knotted to me. I lift up my arm so that he can slot in there.

Daisy ends up snuggled into my chest with Maddox curving around her from behind.

Cleo is still cumming against me. Her little twitches here and there mean that we're going to be knotted a little while longer. Daisy leans into her and they share a kiss. I share a grateful look with Maddox.

I am so content, even as waves of pleasure flow through me. It's more than that. I'm grateful to have my mates with me.

Maddox and I will need to tell the girls soon that we are all mates. Tonight has sped things up a bit. But for now, I can tell that the girls understand that the four of us share a deep connection.

Cleo is spent, and finally my knot eases out of her. She sighs with relief, even though I know how much she enjoyed that.

"You did great, princess." I pull her up higher against me so that we can kiss. My tentacles ease away from her too and move back down to their regular position.

Both Daisy and Cleo start to doze, their eyelids drooping with exhaustion.

"OK, I think it's time to get ready for bed." I announce.

I take both Daisy and Cleo in my arms as Maddox pulls the plug on the tub. Once most of the water is drained, Maddox turns on the shower head. Together, we clean both ourselves and the girls off.

Maddox quickly grabs some fluffy towels as I help the girls out of the tub. Daisy asks for a hair tie and just plops her hair in a bun, saying that she'll have to rewash it in the morning. I make a mental note to have her show me what to do so I can do it correctly next time.

I can't bring myself to sleep away from my mates tonight, so I pass the girls off to Maddox briefly. Pulling the mattresses and blankets from the bunks, I make a makeshift bed in the middle of the main living space of the bus.

Maddox and the girls get into the bed, and I bring them all bottles of water and make sure that no one wants a snack.

Eventually, we all snuggle up together. Cleo and Daisy both curl up on either side of me, Maddox tucking himself in behind Cleo.

Chapter 36

Cleo

I wake up feeling refreshed for the first time in a while. My face is pressed against Nereus' slick and cool chest. Maddox's warm body is laying against me from behind, along with his morning wood.

The temperature difference is actually lovely, keeping me somewhere nice and moderate. I also have my blanket and plushie curled up between me and Nereus.

I really didn't expect mine and Daisy's plan to go down so well last night. I maybe thought that I'd get to kiss Nereus too.

But last night was everything to me. I had *mates* now... or at least I thought so... I remember hearing someone say that alphas only knot their mates. It must have been Flora.

I also knew that there could be groups of mates like this. Take Addison with Hyacinth and Liliana, for example. Besides, Maddox didn't have an alpha knot, and I didn't think he was an alpha. So that meant that the three of us were Nereus' mates.

I know that I shouldn't be getting my hopes up like this. But I also can't help but be excited about finally having my monster mates! And that Daisy was my mate, too?

I can't believe how lucky I am, that I've had one of my mates with me this whole time. No wonder we have always been so close.

Snuggling into Nereus a little more, I can't help but feel so secure with him too. One of his tentacles wraps around me reassuringly and I let out a little sigh. Maddox snuggles in closer behind me too.

Opening my eyes, I see Daisy looking back at me. Her eyes reflect the morning light streaming in, her hair shimmering golden. I didn't realize how close we were, she's snuggled into Nereus' other side. Daisy reaches out her hand to me and I let go of my plushie to hold her.

"Good morning, pretty girl." Daisy whispers, and I feel a warmth blossom through me.

"Morning," I whisper back. "I think I would call last night a success."

Daisy holds in a giggle.

"I really like them." She says.

"So do I" I agree. "Did we accidentally get monster boyfriends?"

Daisy grins. "And human girlfriends... I hope."

"And human girlfriends." I confirm, squeezing her hand reassuringly.

We both blush and Daisy lifts herself up a bit. She leans across Nereus to kiss me, just a soft peck that leaves me wanting more.

"Fuck, my pussy is *aching*." Daisy exclaims.

I frown at her pain. Shifting a little, I realize that I am the same.

"Ouch," I hiss at the movement.

Moving to sit up as well, I notice that I'm trapped by Maddox's heavy arm.

"I'm stuck," I giggle to Daisy.

Playfully sticking her tongue out at me, she gets up to use the bathroom. Abandoning me to our boyfriends.

I wriggle to get comfy again, but the movement just rubs me up against Maddox's hard cock pressed into my back. Maddox groans, holding me firmly against him as he grinds into me in his sleep. I would eagerly grind back into him, but my sore pussy says that I can't handle that right now.

Wriggling some more, I turn so that I am facing him. Cupping his muzzle, I call him until he wakes up. Maddox is confused and horny. Nereus turns, awake now too, pulling me up against his front. He calmly tells Maddox that Daisy and I will be too sore for any funny business today.

Maddox sheepishly grins, and I watch as his cock softens before my eyes. He clearly realizes that it's not the right time.

"Good boy," Nereus tells him.

I press myself back into Nereus, all snuggly once more.

But when Daisy leaves the bathroom, I hop up quickly to use it myself.

Chapter 37

D_aisy_

The guys are awake when I come back into the room and switch places with Cleo. I grab a sweater from our bunk to throw on before joining them in bed again.

I don't want to be giving them any ideas this morning. My pussy was throbbing, and I was going to need a little longer to recover. Especially if I was going to be dancing tonight.

Just when I was about to snuggle back in with the boys, a knock sounds on the door.

"Fuck," Nereus says. "We're probably due on the road soon."

"Oh, I can get it." I say, looking down at my sweater. It's mostly covering my important parts.

Nereus gives me a look that says 'you absolutely will not'. He picks up his discarded shirt off the floor and tosses it on. Nereus opens the door a crack, peering out.

"I guess it's kind of useful that he doesn't have to wear pants," I tease. Sitting back in our makeshift bed, I pull Maddox's head into my lap to stroke his hair. I do drape a blanket over Maddox's hips though, just in case someone comes in.

Nereus is speaking in a low voice, but I can just make out him saying. "Yeah, we had a bit of a rager last night. We just need 20 to tidy up a bit before we can get on the road. No problem, yeah, you got it. One sec."

Nereus comes back in and writes a note, grabbing some cash to go with it. "Here, if you could pick this stuff up, we'll be ready to go by the time you're back. Thanks, dude."

He comes back in, locking the door behind him just as Cleo comes out of the bathroom.

"OK, let's get dressed." Nereus calls out. "I'll tidy up our stuff from last night and put the bunks back together."

Maddox sighs dramatically from my lap.

"But I was getting my hair stroked." He whines, making me chuckle.

I get up, moving to the bunks and pulling out some panties, leggings, and a sports bra.

"Are we driving for long today? I can't remember." I ask out loud.

"Not too far," Nereus says. He slides the mattress and sheets in next to me as soon as I shut the drawer. "We're just going to the human side of this city."

"Oh, good. I really need some time to do my hair properly."

"Me too." Cleo bemoans, pulling out some clothes for herself. "I feel sticky and gross."

I nod, agreeing. I overhear Nereus whispering to Maddox. "We need to get better at the aftercare."

I have to hold in my giggle at how adorable they are. But I'm also pleased that the guys aren't thinking of this as a once off thing. Especially as I seem to be the last one to get to fuck Nereus' cock. That hardly seems fair.

I slip on my clothes and clean up the bar stuff from last night. Just when I'm finishing up, there's another knock at the door.

Nereus rushes past me before I can get to it. He comes back with a tray of coffee cups and a bag of breakfast food. I watch as he pulls out one of the sandwiches and a cup, heading to the driver's door. He chats briefly with the gargoyle, handing him the food and drink.

It was actually really sweet of him to think to do that. Nereus may seem like a bit of an asshole, but he's actually very kind and caring.

Chapter 38

M*addox*

After breakfast, Nereus and Daisy both went off to do their own thing. But Cleo grabbed her e-reader and snuggled up next to me on the couch. I had pulled her in close.

I scroll on my phone while she reads, enjoying the relaxing feeling of contentment.

Cleo turns to face me, sitting up on her knees and clutching her e-reader to her chest.

"What's up?" I ask, seeing the question behind her bright blue eyes, and the way she bites her lip.

"Umm... I'm kind of nervous to ask you what I want to ask."

"I promise I won't make fun of you." I say, and I mean it too.

"Well, I was thinking about it this morning, and then I thought maybe we would talk about it over breakfast. But no one said anything." Cleo worries at the ties of her dress.

"It's alright, you can say it to me."

"Well, just promise you won't think I'm stupid if I'm completely wrong."

"Promise."

Cleo still takes another few seconds before she leans in closer and whispers. "Are we all mates?"

I'm shocked by her astuteness. Leaning back, I search her face.

"Sorry, that was stupid." She sits back on her heels, a look of defeat on her face. Shit.

"No, come here." I pull Cleo onto my lap. "Yes, we're mates."

"Really?!" Her eyes light up as she giggles.

"Really." I hold her close. "We didn't say anything be-cause we didn't want to rush you girls into something that you're not familiar with. But Nereus and I know, which means that we need to tell Daisy."

I look up to see Nereus standing over us.

"I'm glad to see you're happy about the news." Nereus leans down, pulling Cleo into a kiss. She happily sighs when he moves away.

"I'll tell Daisy." He says, heading towards the bunk that Daisy is currently in.

Daisy

A gentle knock sounds on the wall next to my bunk. Cleo wouldn't be bothered to knock, so it must be Nereus or Maddox.

I pause the TV show on the little screen and open the curtain to see Nereus bending down.

"Can I join you?" He surprises me by saying. I eagerly scoot over, happy to get some cuddle time with the Kraken. It was getting warm in here, anyway.

Nereus easily fits into the space, considering it was once his bunk. I snuggle into his open arms.

"What are we watching?" He asks.

"Oh, it's a baking contest show that the human's have. It's pretty popular, and always super wholesome. Want me to go back to the start of the episode?" I lean up a little to look at him while we talk.

"No, that's good. I'm happy to watch from here." Nereus fluffs up the pillow behind himself and gets settled in properly. I am so content to snuggle in and hit play on my comfort show.

By the end of the episode, Nereus has really gotten into it. I giggle as we argue about whether the winning croquembouche should have won. Nereus disagrees with the judges, but I agree with their decision. If he had watched the start, he wouldn't have missed Tim's flan failure.

Nereus huffs, deciding to tickle me instead. I wriggle away, backed into the wall. Our tickles quickly turn to kissing, but then Nereus breaks away.

"I need to tell you something." I'm surprised by his change in demeanor. I sit up, crossing my legs beneath me at his serious tone.

"OK..." I say.

Nereus sits up a little too, so that we're at eye level. I look into his stormy green eyes, waiting for him to speak.

"It's something that I'm a bit nervous to say, if I'm being honest. But I also don't want to keep it from you either."

I can feel my anxiety rising as he pauses for a moment. What would Nereus be nervous to say?

"We're mates. You, me, Cleo, Maddox... we're all mates with one another."

My mind is reeling, and I don't say anything for a moment. I'm happy though, I realize. Last night was so perfect, and I don't think that I would ever want to be with anyone else now.

"How do you know for certain?" I ask. It probably doesn't give Nereus the reassurance that he needs. But I need to know if it's true, and not some wishful thinking.

"It's your scent." Nereus says. "I'm an alpha, and alphas can smell our mate's omega scents. You can only scent your own mate. I've known about Maddox since the day I met him. But I didn't realize about you until the first day of tour, and Cleo was even later."

"Is that what that is?" I ask him. "I had only ever been able to smell Cleo like that. But then I could smell Maddox, and you too, and it was so confusing to me."

"Yeah, probably." Nereus says, stroking my leg tentatively.

"So we're all like Flora and Sebastian?" I ask, earning a nod from Nereus. "But there's *four* of us."

"Yeah," Nereus chuckles. "That's not too weird for monsters. I mean, look at Addison and her mates."

I nod to myself, picturing the three women who were mated to each other.

"My dad is going to freak," I realize.

"Fuck," Nereus sighs. "I don't think that I'd mentally gotten as far as family... My dad is going to love you, though. My mom on the other hand is super protective. Although, she *does* have a soft spot for Maddox."

"Does she know about him?" I ask.

"No, I kept it to myself until I told Maddox a couple days ago."

"Wait, hold up." Was I understanding him correctly? "You didn't tell Maddox for *six years*?!"

"It will make sense when you hear the full story, OK? I promise it was for the best."

"I wonder if he'll agree with that." I am eager to see my minotaur and make sure that he's OK. He had to deal with this news on his own.

"Wow," I continue. "I just had such a visceral response to protect Maddox there. It's weird, how connected I feel with you both. With Cleo, it was a transition from our friendship, but we've always been close. But with you and Maddox, I don't know. It's just developed so quickly, but also so strongly."

I sigh, lost in my own thoughts.

"I'm sorry that I just sprung this on you." Nereus says. "It's OK if you need some time to think about things. Some people decide not to be with their mates, and tha—"

"I'm going to stop you right there." I say, placing a finger on his lips. "I'm so fucking happy that you're my mate. That all three of you are."

"You don't *seem* happy." Nereus says, the sound of his voice muffled by my finger on his lips.

"I'm just processing." I sit back to think on it some more. "Does Cleo know?"

"Cleo literally just figured it out and asked Maddox. It's why the timing of me coming in here was so odd. Maddox was surprised that she had figured it out, but I wasn't."

I smile, shaking my head. "People underestimate Cleo, but she is so emotionally intelligent."

"I can tell," he agrees. "But I can also tell that she's very sensitive."

"For sure," I agree.

This is real life, right? I really have three mates? I've truly found my partners for life. And one of them even has tentacles? It all hits me at one.

"Holy shit," I say, moving to straddle Nereus. "We're *mates.*"

I kiss him, putting all my joy and feelings into it as our lips move together.

"My alpha is a hot, sexy, tentacle monster."

Nereus lifts a tentacle, wrapping it around my waist to prove my point.

"Fuck," Nereus says, pulling me against him. "Call me that again."

Giggling, I think to tease him, but the look on his face has different words coming out of my mouth.

"My alpha."

Nereus' hands move up to cup my face. "Always," he says. "I will always be your alpha. I will protect you and care for you."

"That sounds amazing," I let out a content sigh.

I feel myself relax in a way that I never have before. I'm always worried about looking after Cleo, or my career, or anything else really. But Nereus is sitting here and telling me that I'm looked after. That Cleo is looked after too.

"Let's go hang out with our mates." I say, opening the curtain and climbing out of the bunk.

Letting Nereus follow me, I move into the main living space. Maddox and Cleo are chatting, cuddled up on the couch together. Cleo jumps up when she sees me.

"Did he tell you?" She asks me, her big blue eyes hopeful.

At my nod, she jumps up and down, squealing, before pulling me into a hug. I can't believe this is the first time I'm thinking of this, but this is monumental for Cleo. She has wanted to find somewhere that she belongs for so long now.

"I love you, Cleo." It's not something we haven't said to each other a million times. But it is the first time that I've said it and meant it in a romantic way.

"Me too." Cleo kisses me, our tears mixing together.

Neither Maddox or Nereus look confused at our emotional response to the news, both smiling at us with affection. I kiss Cleo one more time before moving to Maddox on the couch.

Straddling him, I rest one hand on his neck, the other on his muzzle.

"So I guess I'm going to be sitting on my favorite seat for quite a while." I say.

Maddox chuckles. "Are you happy about it?"

"I'm over the moon." I lean closer to him, speaking into his ear. "I'm really looking forward to getting to know you better. I'm so happy that you're my mate, my good boy."

Maddox huffs out a little mewling sound of happiness, nuzzling into my neck. I turn to see Nereus and Cleo sitting down next to us, having had their own little conversation about the news.

I rest my head on Maddox's chest, cuddling closer and enjoying the conversation.

Chapter 39

M*addox*

My butt is numb from sitting on the floor for so long, I can't even move my tail anymore. But I wouldn't dare move. Cleo sits above me on the couch, happily braiding my mane over and over.

I love the feeling of her nails on my scalp as she combs through my hair. She's basically just grooming me, and I fucking love it.

It's been a couple days since we told the girls that we were mates, and we've been living in domestic bliss. We've all settled into a nice little routine.

We set up our makeshift bed on the floor every night and pack it up again before anyone notices the next morning. Most importantly before the driver gets here.

Our trips have been pretty short of late, so our driving has been mostly during the days. That's when the four of us get to sit and chat, getting to know each other better. We share about our families, and our lives together.

Daisy and Cleo have told us all about how they lived together, and about their lifestyle of teaching dance classes and sharing their apartment.

I was pretty upset when they told us that they had decided to move out of their home for this tour. That they had packed all their things away in a storage unit. While I knew that the girls weren't technically homeless, it still didn't sit well with me that they didn't have a home.

Nereus certainly agreed, saying that we will all be living together after the tour, that we will make sure that they are cared for. That wasn't too unexpected for me, but I was surprised at how the girls didn't bristle at that. It seems like they're settling in quite well to having an alpha take care of them.

Things weren't as easy financially for dancers, I had learned. While they got paid well for going on tour, that's all they get paid for. Whereas Nereus and I are on all of Sebastian's recordings, so we were making good money from royalties. Not to mention, we make bank on our performance fees too.

It makes me happy to know that my mates were going to be provided for now.

We haven't had sex since that first night, to give the girls a couple of days to recover. They had to dance every night, and that took a toll on their bodies anyway. We have been making out, however. And plenty of orgasms have been had between us all.

No one has brought up a mating ceremony yet. It's still early days, and we had yet to tell anyone about the bond outside of our foursome. But we were eventually going to have to share it with Flora and Sebastian.

After tonight, we were due a full week off between shows to rest up. Flora and Sebastian were jetting off to the beach on vacation, so we wouldn't be seeing them until they came back.

My head empties out again as Cleo's nails scratch against my scalp. Time for another round of braids, I'm sure. Nereus sits across from us, drinking a cup of coffee and scrolling on his phone. Daisy is on the other side of the couch, folded over as she paints her toe nails.

"I think we should tell Flora and Sebastian tonight." I say, breaking the peaceful silence.

"Shit!" Daisy scowls at me as she cleans up her mistake. She missed her nail completely, painting her toe. "I was trying to concentrate!"

I can't help but get a little excited at her annoyance. She will probably use that as some sort of reason to make me squirm later.

"Yeah, that's fair." Nereus says. "Especially considering that one of you is probably going to go into heat soon."

That's true. I wonder who will be first?

Cleo leans forward, her breath warming my ear.

"What does he mean?" she whispers.

I turn to see a tight look of concern on Cleo's face. One glance at Daisy shows her confusion too.

"I'm sorry," Nereus pipes in. "I thought you knew what that meant. I forget sometimes how different humans really are.

"Going into heat is an exclusively omega thing. You will get very hot and extremely aroused, more than you can even imagine.

"It won't go away until I knot you."

"Ooh, that sounds fun!" Cleo chirps. I want to tell her that it can be, but it can also be unbearable, from what I've heard. But maybe it's best not to say that right now.

"So... are we telling Flora and Sebastian before or after the show tonight?" Daisy asks.

"Well they're flying out right after, so probably before." Cleo answers.

Nereus and I leave them to it, the girls choreographing our evening. They text Flora to hang out with them on the next pit stop.

Chapter 40

N_ereus_

Sebastian, Maddox and I sit around the table in our bus, playing cards. It's just like old times, for a couple hours at least.

"We have something to tell you." I cut to the chase. Although, I decide to ease him into it a bit too. "Maddox and I..."

Maddox's hand is resting on the table, and I take it in mine. He presses his leg against me, and I can feel his nervous tremor.

"Well, we haven't completed the bond yet. But we're mates."

Sebastian blinks at me blankly for a second, almost to make sure it isn't a joke. Once he realizes that I'm serious, his face breaks into a grin.

"Holy shit, guys. That's amazing!" Sebastian hops out of his seat to hug us both.

"You're really not mad about it?" Maddox asks as he and Sebastian hug. My heart breaks for my mate, he hadn't told me how unsure he was about this. It's probably why he brought up telling them, to get it over with.

"Of course I'm not. I'm so happy for you both."

Maddox visibly relaxes, and I pull him back against me. His warm and soft body comforts me.

"There's more though," I add, before we get too off track.

"More... mates?" Sebastian wonders. I nod, and he continues. "Wow. First Addison and now you guys. I swear, I don't understand how you can handle two mates. It's a lot of focus just protecting one."

Deciding to be brave, I say, "Three, actually."

Sebastian takes another second to process, mentally doing some math by the look of it.

"The girls," I answer for him. "Cleo and Daisy. They're our mates."

Sebastian pulls us in for a hug, together this time. "I'm so happy for you guys. They needed some strong mates to look out for them, and I couldn't have wished for anyone better than you two for that."

I'm surprised by how emotional Sebastian's words make me. Maddox is visibly crying.

"Thanks man," he says, sniffling.

"So I guess they're telling Flora right now?"

"Yeah," I say. We all get back into our seats, the card game forgotten.

"She's going to be so excited for them. Thank fuck we're going away tonight. We can give you guys some peace." Sebastian says. "What are your plans for the week off? Will you all be doing anything nice?"

"I have something booked." I say, enjoying the look of surprise on Maddox's face.

Chapter 41

Cleo

The past couple days have been the best of my life.

I've always wanted people that I could call my own. I had that with Daisy as friends. But I always had this voice in the back of my head that Daisy could find some guy to leave me hanging for.

My mom did everything to give me the best life she could. She kept me in dance classes when I know that we couldn't afford it. When Mom passed, I was nineteen and alone.

Daisy's dad let me move in with them until she and I were able to afford our own place. Ever since then, I've been searching for that sense of belonging.

Having mates that were connected to you on a biological level had stood out to me. They would always be there for me.

Telling Flora was making me nervous though, and I cling to Daisy as we walk to the bus.

"What's up, babe?" Daisy strokes my cheek, and it fills me with warmth.

"I'm a little scared of telling Flora. But when I say it out loud I realize that's stupid. Because of course Flora will be happy for us… right?" I think I just need some reassurance.

"Of course, honey. Don't worry, I'll tell her. OK? You don't need to say anything unless you want to."

She kisses me on the forehead, sending a tingle down to my toes.

"Besides," Daisy continues. "You're forgetting that we're here to share *good* news."

I let out a giggle, sufficiently cheered up. Daisy was right, this was good news that we were sharing. I should be excited.

Daisy knows me so well. She knows exactly what to say when I get a little anxious about something.

When we get to the bus, she squeezes my hand gently.

"I love you." She tells me. I smile up at her, taking in her beautiful eyes, her wild hair. Those three words reassure me. I am so happy to have the love of my best friend, and for her to be my mate too.

Flora squeals, opening up the bus door to us.

"Yay! I'm so excited for a few hours with my girls!"

She wraps us both up in a hug and we head inside. We sit on either side of her on the couch, asking Flora how she is.

"I'm good. But I need this beach break. I'm exhausted and I want to sleep in a real bed. What are you girls doing for the week?" Flora asks.

"We're not really sure yet, but this is a perfect segue into something that we wanted to talk to you about." Daisy starts. Flora nods, waiting for her to continue. "We um... well, we found our mates."

"We?" Flora asks, looking to me for confirmation.

"Yeah, Daisy and I are kind of together now?" My nerves get to me and I sound like I'm asking a question.

"Wait... so you're each other's mates?" Flora tries to wrap her head around it, her golden brows fused together. "With who?"

She directs her question to me, but I can't speak. I stare at her, chewing on my lip. Daisy jumps in to save me, stealing Flora's attention.

"With Nereus and Maddox." Daisy says, simply.

Flora squeals again, pulling us into a hug on either side of her. "I didn't know you could have *three* mates?!"

"I know, me neither!" Daisy explains.

"Oh my God, Maddox and *Nereus*? I love this for you! Wait, oh my god, the tentacles. I know we've talked about them already, but have you had *sex*?"

I giggle at my friend's enthusiasm, feeling relieved.

"The tentacles are *amazing*," I tell her as Daisy nods vigorously.

Daisy chimes in, "but, like, so is Maddox."

"I'm obsessed with playing with his mane at the moment." I explain. "He's so cozy for snuggles."

We chat about all the details, my chest warm from the love of my friends and my mate.

Chapter 42

Maddox

Nereus and I wait side stage for our girls. Tonight is different.

When they come off, sweating and cheering, they have their usual hug. But tonight they kiss, in full view of the crew.

They're so pretty, blond bubble braids and curly red pigtails. They wear sparkly body suits and furry boots, all in Flora's signature pastels.

When they break apart, I gesture for them to come join us. Nereus is chatting to a stage hand about some wires that were placed improperly the night before.

Daisy and Cleo wrap their arms around me, one on either side. Leaning down I give each of them a kiss. Cleo first, her warm body pliable beneath me. Daisy takes control, her kiss feels like a claiming.

Coldness blooms on my left as Cleo moves away, probably to Nereus. But I am all eyes for Daisy, who pulls away before our kiss becomes a little too much for public consumption. She stays in my arms though, cupping my cheek and stroking the fur there.

"You're going to do great tonight," she tells me.

Daisy leans in for one more kiss until Nereus crowds her from behind. She turns to him, and he gives her a chaste kiss. But Nereus can also smell her arousal, so perhaps he didn't want to push her too much.

"You girls try not to have too much fun in that dressing room tonight." Nereus teases them, Cleo still pressed tight against him. "Especially because we won't have long before we need to leave."

I can't help my grin, watching the look of surprise on the girl's faces.

"Are we going somewhere?" Cleo sweetly asks, her blue eyes alight with excitement.

"Go pack your bags and we'll catch you after the show at the bus." Nereus says. "It's a surprise. Even Maddox doesn't know where we're going."

Daisy snuggles back into my chest. "This is exciting," She says. "Want me to pack your bag too?"

Relieved, I nod. I wasn't sure when I was going to get the chance to do that.

"And Nereus," I tell her. "I bet he's forgotten that he'll need to pack, too."

The girls kiss us both again in goodbye. Excited for their surprise, they skip off towards their dressing room together.

Instead of coming over to me like I expect, Nereus grabs a trusted member of the crew. He slips him a bill, whispering something to him.

"What's wrong?" I ask at his suspicious behavior.

"It might be nothing, but I could have sworn that Daisy's scent shifted a little. I asked Rob to discreetly make sure that the girls get back to the bus OK. I'm worried that she's going to go into heat soon."

Nereus rubs at the back of his head, his brows furrowed. I worry for him and all his responsibilities with three mates. I place a chaste kiss on his cheek.

"If you've only smelled a shift, then nothing is going to change for the next few hours." I assure him. "We can push through the journey to wherever we're going. Which I'm sure, knowing you, is somewhere safe and secluded anyway."

Nereus nods, absentmindedly stroking my mane.

"Yeah, you're right." He agrees. "Let's just focus on getting through the set tonight, and then I can make sure that you're all tucked in for the week."

Chapter 43

Daisy

Cleo's soft mouth presses against mine, sending a pulse of pleasure straight to my pussy.

"I'm sorry," she says, pulling away. "I'm too excited to go pack."

Giggling, I turn her around smacking her ass.

"I wish we had time to go shopping!" She bemoans, leaning back against me in nothing but her thong.

"For sure," I agree, watching us in the mirror. I can't help but cup her boobs. "I have no idea what to pack."

"Well, we barely have anything with us. And something tells me we'll probably spend the whole time naked any-way..."

Cleo turns to me, leaning forward and taking my nipple into her mouth. Heat blossoms in my core from that move, and I can't help the loud moan that escapes me.

"Shh," Cleo smiles, pulling away from me to put on her sweatpants. "Come on, let's go pack."

We quickly get dressed and head toward the bus. I can't stop looking at Cleo as we walk, just knowing how sexy she is under that puffer coat and sweatpants. How I want to run my hands over the globe of her ass again soon. Maybe packing can wait.

But once we get to the bus, Cleo is all action. I remember how I told Maddox that I would pack for him and Nereus too. So I get changed into a travel outfit, taking off my makeup, and pack our luggage.

Cleo gets ready too, and spends the same amount of time packing her own bag as it takes me to do the other three.

Moving the last suitcase to the front of the bus, I plop down on the couch to join Cleo. She is already curled up there with her e-reader.

Realizing how exhausted I actually am, I put on an episode of my favorite baking show. Cleo puts her head in my lap and I find myself stroking her hair while she reads.

I'm almost finished with my episode by the time the guys make it onto the bus. They wear matching wolfish grins on their faces, fueled by post-show adrenaline.

Cleo hops up, all excited. She abandons her e-reader on the couch and jumps right into Nereus' open arms.

"Are we leaving now? Where are we going?" She yaps excitedly.

"Let's all use the restroom, and then we can go." Nereus answers her. "We're traveling by car so you won't be able to go again for a while."

"Ooh a *car*," Cleo chimes, hopping down and rushing to the bathroom. Nereus chuckles after her.

"Cleo loves surprises." I inform him. "You could literally do anything now and she'll be impressed."

Nereus sidles in next to me on the couch, Maddox doing the same on my other side.

"Wait, are you watching this without me?" Nereus asks with an offended look, gesturing at the TV.

I can't help but laugh at his reaction. "Am I not supposed to now?"

"No." He says, indignant. "That's *our* show now."

"Well, I promise not to watch it without you again." I say, cupping his face in my hand. "I'll even re-watch this episode with you, OK?"

He huffs, saying that it's the least I could do. I hold in my giggle, not having the heart to tell him that they canceled this show three years ago. We were watching reruns anyway.

Maddox pulls me back against him, settling me on his lap. "I missed you," he says under his breath, nuzzling my neck with his muzzle and sniffing me.

I'm about to tease him for it when I realize that I missed him too, both of them. I'm feeling a little weird, and I want my mates around me. I turn my head a little, kissing the bridge of Maddox's muzzle.

He smells particularly good, like sweetened chestnuts. I find myself kissing him, twisting so that I'm straddling him, grinding against his length. Cleo calls out to me, snapping me out of my haze.

"Come on, Daisy. You can kiss him in the car! Let's go."

Once we're all finally ready, Nereus walks us to the back of the lot. He and Maddox carry all of our suitcases. Down by the back gate, a large limo is waiting for us.

Cleo squeals, hopping in the back seat. I follow her in as the guys sort out our luggage. It doesn't take long for us to get settled, the car moving away. With the tinted windows, I can't see where we're going.

Cleo snuggles in next to Maddox with her e-reader and he scrolls on his phone, picking out the music that we're listening to and telling us about each song he's picking.

I sit next to Nereus, cuddled into his arm as we re-watch the episode from earlier. He has his hand on my thigh and a tentacle wrapped around my calf.

Nereus is pretty invested in the show, but I can't help being distracted by his hand. He's close enough to be able to cup my pussy, just the thought of him doing that is more than I can handle. I squirm a little in my seat.

"You OK?" Nereus asks, running his thumb over me soothingly.

I shake my head with a little whine. I'm so horny, my pussy throbbing. Nereus looks to Maddox before coming back to me.

"Remember when I told you about going into heat?" He asks me, his voice gentle.

I move my head to the side, remembering the conversation. My breaths come quick as I start to panic.

"Is it happening?" I ask. "I don't want it to happen *here.*"

Nereus shushes me, "It's alright, sweetheart. You're not going to feel much more than this for a few hours, and our drive is shorter than that. OK?"

Nereus shifts us so that his arm is around me now, pressing me against his chest.

"Are you sure?" I squirm again as another wave of desire hits me.

I can see Cleo moving to join me, but Nereus shakes his head at her.

My body is getting warmer, and I'm grateful for my cool skinned Kraken beneath me.

"I promise," he tells me. "Don't worry. We'll be in our nice safe spot before you properly go into heat."

Stripping myself of my sweater, I snuggle back into Nereus in just my tank top. That helps with my temperature.

Is this really going to get worse?

Chapter 44

*M*addox

Daisy is flushed, pressed up against our alpha. His cool skin will only be able to help for so long. I hope we get to where we're going in time.

I trust Nereus implicitly, but I can't help my rising anxiety for Daisy.

Cleo's tiny hand touches my cheek, getting my attention.

"Nereus said she'll be OK," she says, stroking my face.

"I know. I'm just a worrier." I answer.

Not knowing where we were going or how close we were to getting there was starting to make me more unsettled than excited.

"Come here," Cleo says, shifting a bit further away so that I can rest my head on her.

Curling up, I nuzzle my head into her pillowy boobs while she strokes my mane.

My body starts to relax, and I can't help the almost purr-like sound that escapes me.

Nereus

I'm the only one to stay awake for the entire journey. My mates all fell asleep a couple of hours ago. Maddox rests his head in Cleo's lap as she reclines, her hands buried in his mane.

Daisy is tucked into my chest, but luckily her temperature hasn't risen too much.

The driver gave me the ten minutes to arrival signal not too long ago. So I knew that I was going to have to wake up my mates, but they all looked so peaceful.

I am beyond grateful that we managed to keep it together without anyone going into heat until this week. Now that it was happening to Daisy, the others will be close behind. Judging by the shift in Maddox's scent, he could be next. Cleo still smells normal, at least.

I had timed it so that groceries would be delivered and put away for us by the time we get in. So I should be able to give Daisy some much needed attention as soon as we get there. I don't think that she's going to last much longer, and I've already resigned myself to the idea that I am not going to get any sleep tonight.

The driver flashes the light to signal five minutes until arrival.

"It's time to wake up, sweetheart." I stroke Daisy's cheek.

Stretching out a tentacle, I curl it around Maddox's leg. "We're almost there. Time to wake up."

Everyone groggily moves to sitting, except Daisy who stays snuggled up against me. That's fine, I can carry her in, I just want her to be comfortable.

Now that Cleo has woken up a bit, she is bouncing in her seat, excited to see where I've brought them.

I hope she isn't disappointed. Cleo is the most beautiful when her face lights up with joy. That's what I want for her.

Chapter 45

Cleo

The car comes to a stop, the engine clicking off. I move for the door right away, the driver getting there seconds before me. I think I nearly hop into his arms in my rush to get out of the car.

I'm faced with a densely wooded space that looks a little creepy in the dark. When I turn, I see a giant log cabin, the porch lights casting a glow of its shape.

There's also a lake shore, the lights set up around it reflecting off its calm surface. I sigh with contentment, the crisp air filling my lungs.

Maddox joins me and I grin, sharing in the high. He sighs just like I did, taking in the beautiful area. It's pretty cold, my body shivering. Maddox wraps me in my coat that I abandoned in the car.

Nereus comes out next, Daisy in his arms. He's wrapped her sweater around her shoulders, but that's hardly enough to warm her. Moving back to them, I see that Daisy is clammy and sweaty, some of her curls stuck to her face. I stroke them away, clearing her face and Daisy sighs, her eyes fluttering open.

"Oh, it's so nice and cold out here." She says.

I look worriedly to Nereus, but he assures me that this is normal and everything is OK. I try to believe him.

"The house is beautiful," I tell him.

"It's where I come when I want to get out of the city."

I can understand that, especially with the big lake. I'm sure that's perfect for my Kraken.

"Wait, you own this place? Why have I never been here?" Maddox asks, sounding a little put out.

"It was a private space. Somewhere I hoped you would join me one day, though." Nereus presses a kiss to Maddox's forehead.

By this point, the driver has moved all our suitcases and things up to the porch. So we head that way ourselves. I let the others go inside, but I wait on the porch for a minute, my mind processing things.

My mate owns a secret house? Meaning that he owns more than one? I could probably come here whenever I wanted.

I take in another deep lungful of fresh air and look up at the sky full of stars. We must be somewhere pretty remote, the sky filled with beautiful twinkling lights.

"You coming in?" Nereus' low voice calls from behind me. He moves to join me out on the porch.

"Yeah," I say. But I make no move to leave, still staring at the stars.

Nereus strokes my hair, giving me the space to speak.

"I'm very grateful, that's all. I don't have much, and this is a lot for me. But I'm so very grateful for it."

"Come here, princess." I turn, snuggling into his chest. "Everything I have is yours, now. I promise that I will always look after you."

I realize that I'm crying into his chest, leaving a cooling wet patch on his coat.

"I love you." He says to me, pulling away so that he can look into my eyes.

Oh, shit. I sniffle, my heart warm.

"I love you too." I mean it.

It's not because Nereus has a nice house or anything like that. I love his soul, how he looks out for his mates, how we have fun together.

I smile through my tears, Nereus wiping them away.

"Come inside." He says. "Come home."

I follow my mate into the warm and inviting cabin.

Chapter 46

D^*aisy*

A heavy tiredness consumes me as I drift in and out of sleep. Maddox's muscular, warm arms wrap around me as Nereus passes me off.

"So warm," I whine.

"I know, just give me a sec."

A flash of cold hits me as Maddox opens what I think is a fridge. I doze off again until I'm settled onto something soft and plush. Something rigid presses against my mouth.

"Here," Maddox strokes my hair. "Take a sip."

I want to tell him not to touch my hair, but the sticky sweaty feeling tells me it's already ruined. Taking the bottle from his hand, the cool condensation feels fantastic. I take a sip. It's some sort of tasty electrolyte drink, and I guzzle half the bottle down.

"God, I needed that." I didn't realize how thirsty I had been.

"You poor thing," Maddox says, leaning over me.

I haven't felt that horny since I fell asleep in the car. Which was weird, wasn't it? I thought the whole point of the heat was that I would get super horny.

But looking at Maddox now, braced over me, his face lined with concern. I feel my pussy wake up again. Maddox takes the bottle away from me, setting it down somewhere behind him. When he makes to move away, I can't let that happen. I pull him back onto me, and he nearly crushes me, scrambling to keep himself up.

I chuckle, pushing him back so he lays flush against the cushions. We're on a couch, I realize as I climb onto him. I grind on his cock through our clothes, he even has his coat on still. It feels so good, and I can feel him hardening beneath me.

"Good boy," I tell him as he gets harder. "That's it. Give me something to rub against."

I place my hands on his chest, my eyes hooded with lust as I grind on him, the pleasure too intense to stop.

"Fuck, this feels so good." I tell him.

Maddox whines, holding my hips and helping me to press harder against him.

"Yes," I cry out.

"Daisy?" Cleo asks, moving just into my peripheral. I call her to me, pulling her in for a deep kiss as I continue to grind on my minotaur. I'm hit with an onslaught of sensations, my hand fisting in Maddox's shirt.

I pull away from Cleo, a thought striking me.

"Where's my alpha?" I ask.

"He's just checking the house." Cleo tells me, using the time to take off her coat and sweater. "He'll be back in a minute."

Cleo stands before me in her sports bra and leggings. Her cleavage and tiny waist on display.

"Fuck, you're so hot." I ease off of Maddox, setting him free as I tug Cleo onto my lap. She cries out as I cup her boob and pinch her nipple through the fabric.

Pulling down the strap on her bra, I free her boob and take her nipple into my mouth. I look up at Cleo with a smirk. She tastes like vanilla cake batter, and I can't get enough of it.

I lift my own shirt out of the way and reach into my leggings. There's a pool of wetness there, and I rub my clit, pleasure stoking through me as I play with Cleo's boob.

I feel Nereus before I see him, a tentacle wrapping around my neck, pulling my head back and away from Cleo. She is writhing against my leg, but she quickly stops and moves to Maddox when she looks at Nereus.

Cleo settles on Maddox's lap and they grind together. I rub at my clit faster when they start to make out, watching them intently and knowing that I got them both so worked up.

Nereus moves around me, coming into view. Finally, my alpha is here. I continue to work my clit, my orgasm building.

"Look how hot and bothered you are," Nereus says, playing the asshole. "Is that for me?"

I refuse to give in, feeling bratty. I turn my head away from him, watching Cleo and Maddox. Nereus tightens the tentacle around my neck, cutting off my air as he tugs me to look at him again.

"I know it's for me, sweetheart..." He climbs up onto the couch, his tentacles spreading around me. Nereus lifts up his two front tentacles and I realize what he is doing.

I gladly open my mouth to him. My fingers rub my clit hard, slipping around in my mess. I nearly cum at the sight of my alpha's cock. The tentacles covering his knot, but I know it's there. His dark green head leaks a clear liquid that I want to taste.

I stick out my tongue, keeping my mouth open, looking up at my alpha.

He moves forward, engulfing me in his center. I reach up with my spare hand and take his cock in my mouth and my hand. Swirling my tongue around his head, my hand squeezes just above his knot.

Nereus' cock is rigid beneath my touch, and I feel powerful with how hard he is for me. I suck on his head, swirling my tongue and moving my hand up and down his shaft.

I can't concentrate on fingering myself anymore. So I release my clit and use some of my wetness to coat his cock as I use both hands to stroke his shaft. I try to use my mouth to fuck his cock as much as I can fit. I make it down far enough that I can taste myself on him.

"Fuck," I hear him moan above me as I gag on his cock, pushing him as far down my throat as I can.

The tentacle around my neck tightens again and I am pulled back against the couch cushion as he bucks against me. He takes his pleasure from my mouth, and I relax into being used like this, my fingers finding my clit again.

It doesn't take long to find my release, crying out beneath him as I do.

Nereus pulls away, his cock dripping. He wipes away some of the tears that stream down my face from his hard fucking.

"What a good girl you are," he says. Pride flows through me. Some of the haze that I was feeling has gone away now that I've cum, too.

I was still sitting with my hand in my leggings. I quickly remove it, feeling a little weird about the whole situation.

Nereus grips my wrist in a tentacle, lifting my fingers up and sucking on them. The feeling of his rough tongue against my slick fingers is amazing. I moan at the sensation, my hips bucking.

He moves away, pulling off his sweater and revealing his toned torso. Then he helps me to take off my clothes. When he takes off my panties, he sniffs them, making sure that I can see the pleasure in his eyes as he does so.

I move to rub my clit again but a tentacle stops me. Whining, I buck against nothing, needing some friction.

"Cleo," Nereus says, getting her attention. "Come and lick out your mate's pussy."

Cleo quickly kneels on the floor before me.

Chapter 47

Cleo

I quickly follow my alpha's command, kneeling before my mate and licking her clit. She tastes like dark berries and spices. I need more of it.

Tentacles come at us all at once. One slithers up between Daisy and I, entering her pussy and making her cry out.

Another tentacle finds my nipple, pulsing against it just like I love. I can feel one more worming its way between my legs, so I shift to put my ass in the air. It easily slides inside my wet pussy, fucking me quickly.

"Good girl," Nereus says above me. He smacks my ass and It's like a line of electricity shoots from there straight to my clit.

My eyes follow Nereus as he prowls towards Maddox. He pulls him into a claiming kiss, and I can't help but be distracted by them. Glancing up at Daisy, I can see that she's watching them too.

I rest my head against Daisy's thigh so that I can look at the males. She reaches down and rubs her own clit, so I do the same. Pleasure floods me as Nereus' tentacle continues to fuck me.

Nereus flips Maddox over so that his cock is hanging between his legs. Daisy reaches across the small distance to stroke Maddox's cock, making him grunt in pleasure. I love the sounds that my minotaur makes.

I can just barely hold it together, watching Nereus lift Maddox's tail out of the way as he mounts his back. Nereus turns to the side slightly and I can tell it's for the benefit of our view. We watch as he covers his cock in lube, then presses it into Maddox's ass.

My orgasm is so close. The view, my fingers on my clit, the tentacles fucking my pussy and sucking on my nipple...

The noise that Maddox makes is what sends me over the edge, cumming hard.

The tentacle inside my pussy doesn't let up, but the one on my nipple eases off me as I rest forward on Daisy's leg. Daisy cums soon after me, and my eyes flick between Daisy and my other two mates coming together.

"Nereus," I say, becoming a little too sensitive from his tentacle. His attention switches to me as he continues to pound Maddox.

"Are you done, princess?" I nod and his tentacle eases out of me. Daisy continues to writhe beneath me, my breathing heavy. "Good girl, you did so good for us."

Daisy screams as another orgasm racks through her.

"Daisy, get over here." Nereus says. She cries out as he pulls away from her, leaving her empty and wanting.

I move out of the way as Daisy kneels on the couch next to Maddox and Nereus. I climb up onto the couch behind her. It gives me a perfect view of her leaking pussy, her juices smeared all over her legs. My fingers brush against her pussy and sink inside, feeling her clench around them.

"Give me a taste." My alpha commands. I eagerly stretch my hand up and he takes it into his mouth, licking my fingers clean.

"You taste so good, sweetheart." He groans, bucking harder against Maddox. "Do you want to take your Minotaur's cock?"

"Y-yes," Daisy stammers over her words.

"Then get under there," Nereus says, "and let him fuck you."

Maddox

Nereus tells Daisy to get under me and I nearly lose my load at the idea.

She crawls beneath me, but I can't bend to kiss her in this position. She kisses and sucks at my nipples, my dick in her hand. I hiss at how sensitive it is to her touch.

Daisy turns over, getting into position. A tentacle wraps around my dick, guiding me into her slick pussy. She pushes back against me and the tentacle falls away. She's soaking, and I slip inside her easily.

I'm completely at Nereus' mercy, my thrusts timed by his. Something soft presses against my back, and I turn enough to see that Nereus has Cleo in his arms. Her butt grazes against my back as they move. They seem to be kissing, but I can't be sure.

Relaxing to face forward again, Nereus hits a whole new spot inside me. His smaller tentacles fondling and massaging my balls and Daisy meeting my every thrust.

"I need to cum." I desperately hold back the pressure building up inside me. It builds and builds but Nereus ignores me. I can hear him and Cleo kissing.

"Alpha," I call again. "I *really* need to cum. Can I please cum?"

I can feel tears streaming down my face, sweat pouring down my back from the effort.

"Ask your mate. Ask Daisy if you can cum." Nereus finally speaks.

Daisy pushes back against me, fucking me harder.

"Cum in me, please." She whines.

I don't need any more encouragement, the pressure exploding quickly, some of my cum leaking out before my flares expand.

Daisy cries out beneath me, and I cry out too as Nereus quickly pulls out and away from me.

Shifting onto my side, I pull Daisy against me and try to make her more comfortable.

Chapter 48

Nereus

Cleo sits in my lap as we watch Daisy's stomach expand with Maddox's cum.

"I think we're going to need a new couch," I whisper into her ear, earning myself a giggle.

Maddox continues to buck into Daisy, and it's obvious to me now that my minotaur has gone into heat too as he ruts into her.

I wonder if I should be concerned, but Daisy is nearly cross-eyed with the pleasure, and she meets him thrust for thrust.

Guiding my attention back to Cleo, I stroke her hair. "Are you feeling OK?"

"I'm feeling great." She says, smiling up at me, her arms around my neck. "I don't think I'm in heat yet, though."

"Definitely not," I agree, kissing her on the forehead. "I am going to have to knot them both a couple times over the next few days. You too, if you go into heat as well. It's not going to be over tonight."

She nods slowly, processing the information. "I'm tired," she says.

"Let me put you to bed, and then I will look after these two a bit longer."

She yawns as I stand, keeping her in my arms. My cock is no longer at full mast, but I'm definitely still turned on. Not that Cleo can see with my tentacles in the way.

I bring Cleo to the bedroom in the back of the house. It's a space that I had built to fit three Monsters, just in case Maddox and I found a third at some point. It's also the perfect size for two humans and two monsters.

I show Cleo to the bathroom and help her clean up before tucking her into the bed with a kiss. I leave the door to the room open a crack so that I can hear her if she needs anything.

Heading back to the living space, I find Maddox and Daisy still rutting on the couch. I just stand and watch for a minute, completely enthralled with how they move together.

Daisy whimpers, finally slackening against Maddox. He eases off, calming himself to just a thrust here and there.

I sit next to them, shifting myself underneath Daisy. Cooling down my body temperature as much as I can earns me a groan of relief from the pair. Maddox bucks against Daisy again.

"You need to control yourself," I tell him. "You're pushing Daisy too far."

Her stomach is so stretched out. How much of a load was Maddox letting off? I should have made him cum first before letting him cum in one of the girls.

But Daisy seems content. In fact, she looks really into it.

After a few minutes, Maddox finally eases his cock out of Daisy. A torrent of cum flows from her. Maddox is too spent to even notice the mess he's making

I am going to need to call a cleaner to come while we're sleeping. But judging by the way that Daisy is climbing onto me, sleep is still very far away.

She straddles me with Maddox's cum still leaking out of her. It's so fucking hot. She sits up high on my torso and drags me into a deep kiss.

"I want to take my alpha's knot." She says, pulling back.

"Do you now?" I tease. "While you're still full of my omega's cum?"

She nods vigorously, clearly turned on by that thought. I maneuver my front tentacles to the side so I can ease her onto my cock. Daisy cries out with pleasure as I stretch her wide again.

Maddox's cum is more than enough lubricant, and I have to be careful not to pound into her too quickly. I can't forget Maddox next to me either. I pull him to me, wrapping my arm around him and easing a tentacle into his ass.

Daisy clings to us both, one hand on my chest, the other gripping Maddox's arm. She finally moves down a bit further on my cock, and my smaller tentacles play with her clit and her ass. When she gets a bit more comfortable, I let her take control and fuck me however she wants.

Fuck, minotaur cum really is the best lube. I kiss Maddox in gratitude.

"Fuck my ass." Daisy says, piquing both of our attention and breaking our kiss. She's struggling to move as fast as she'd like, so I take over again, pounding upwards.

"Do you want a tentacle in your ass, sweetheart?"

"Yes," she moans. "Then I want you in my ass."

She looks to Maddox as she says it. I try to keep the good enough sense to say, "Let's start with my tentacle and see how you go."

Chapter 49

Daisy

I'm losing my mind with the pleasure. Just when I think I can't take anymore, I find that nothing is *enough*.

Nereus slows our thrusting and I feel a tentacle pressing against my ass. I know that I'm supposed to relax through it, and Maddox's cum lets the tip of Nereus' tentacle easily glide inside of me.

He keeps his thrusts shallow. It feels strange for a moment, until the tickling sensation becomes so much more. Crying out, I start to move myself against Nereus again.

I grip Maddox's arm hard, I want to be fucked by them both at the same time so badly.

"More," I say to Nereus, not that I have gotten used to the first invasion.

Nereus' tiny tentacles suck at my clit and I quickly orgasm through it all. My body is flushed, and full of pleasure. He pauses his thrusting for a bit to give me a breather.

"You're doing so well." He tells me. "Want to keep going?"

"Yes," I moan. "I want both of my males to fuck me at the same time." My voice comes out as a desperate whine.

"We will," Maddox promises. He leans forward to watch where Nereus is fucking my pussy with his cock and my ass with his tentacle.

"Fuck," Maddox sighs as Nereus pushes further in, stretching me even wider.

"Give me a sec," I say as the stretch starts to burn. Nereus strokes my back, praising me until I relax again. Once the burning subsides, Nereus moves against me. I barely see it but I think Nereus is still fucking Maddox in the ass too.

"She's ready," Nereus says. "Make sure you're ready to go when I pull out."

Maddox moves to position behind me, knees on the couch and cock in his hand.

"Ready," he tells Nereus.

Nereus pulls out of my ass and my pussy all at once, which I'm not expecting. I cry out at the empty feeling. But Maddox quickly pushes against my ass and I feel so full from him there already. He holds still against me as Nereus moves to pull my pussy back to his cock.

The pressure is so intense as he fills me, I feel like I'm going to pass out.

"That's it, sweetheart." Nereus eases me down as far as his knot. I whimper from the pleasure as his smaller tentacles stroke at my sensitive clit again.

I lean back against Maddox, letting his soft chest cushion me. Both of my mates praise me as they ease into a tandem fuck. I pant and moan and whimper through it all, feeling so connected to them both.

"I'm going to cum." Nereus tells us and Maddox pulls out of my ass, kissing my shoulder. He continues to fist his cock as Nereus pushes up into me, his knot expanding.

I can see why Maddox couldn't be in my ass for this, Nereus feels like he is everywhere, all at once. The pressure of his knot makes my vision spotty and I cling to his chest to stay upright.

Maddox spews his second load all over us both, my hands becoming slippery against Nereus.

Leaning forward, I rest against Nereus' chest as another orgasm forces its way through me. It's too much, and I stay as still as possible.

Maddox collapses next to us and I drift off to sleep for a while.

I wake up in Nereus' arms as he takes me to the bathroom. They sit me on a bench in the shower, and the stream of water feels glorious.

Nereus does my hair like I taught him, and I'm dried off pretty quickly, my hair plopped in an old t-shirt.

When Nereus lays me on the big bed, I pull Cleo into my arms, falling asleep again before the guys even join us.

Chapter 50

Cleo

The first thing I notice when I wake up is how hot I am. Maddox must be snuggling in behind me. But that's human skin I feel.

It's not that I don't want to cuddle Daisy, but she's so warm. I turn to see Nereus on my other side, holding Maddox. Perfect, Nereus will be cool.

I grab his arm and place my cheek there, finding a temporary reprieve. Nereus wakes up at the contact, caressing my waist with a tentacle.

"I'm so hot," I tell him, in lieu of a good morning.

Nereus wakes Maddox, telling him to go open the balcony door. All the movement in the bed wakes up Daisy.

"What's going on?" Daisy asks.

"Cleo is going into heat." Nereus says, pulling back the covers and lifting me to sit on top of them. Is that what this is? Am I going into heat? I hate it.

"Are you just hot or are you horny too?" Nereus asks me as Maddox gets back into the bed with Daisy now.

A cool breeze hits me from the open doors, making my nipples harden painfully. I look at each of my patient mates waiting for my answer. Maddox's pretty mane and chiseled abs. Daisy with her green eyes reflecting the morning light, her full tits peeking out of the covers. Nereus with his stormy green eyes and cheeky smile.

"Horny, too."

"Come here then, princess." Nereus pulls me into his cold lap, kissing me slowly and sensually. His rough tongue exploring my mouth and creating a wetness between my thighs.

I lose myself in the kiss, content to live in this moment forever. That is, until a small finger slips inside my pussy, setting me alight. Daisy's fingers press and massage against my g-spot, building up the pressure of an incoming orgasm.

Her fingers are replaced by a tentacle, and Maddox leans around Daisy to kiss me. I'm the center of all their attention as Nereus fucks me. My sleepy brain is quickly blissed out, my orgasm washing over me in a wave of tingles.

"Good girl," Daisy tells me, pulling me in for a kiss, then working her way down to play with my nipples.

Nereus pulls me back against him, his cock easing into me from behind. "Good girl, you're doing so great." He whispers in my ear, with so much more praise as he fucks me.

Daisy continues to attend to my boobs, and Maddox leans over her, kissing me with so much love and affection. It's such a sweet and tender moment.

It doesn't take long for Nereus to grunt, his knot pushing inside me as he fills me with his cum. I lean back against him, my head drooping as I fall back to sleep.

<h1 style="text-align:center">Chapter 51</h1>

M*addox*

Nereus cleaned up Cleo in the shower while Daisy and I made breakfast. It was so nice to cook in a big kitchen again after being in the bus for so long. It was also just fun to be cooking with my mate.

I was embarrassed to discover that the couch had been cleaned. Which meant that Nereus had someone over to clean up my cum. Although I do appreciate that I didn't have to do it myself.

We sit at the table now, eating the eggs, bacon, pancakes, and fruit that Daisy and I made. We chat a little over our food, discussing how we want to spend our day.

After breakfast, we go for a stroll on the lake front. It's peaceful, and Nereus has these nice big deck chairs out. So Cleo and I curl up in one with Nereus and Daisy in another.

"It might be a good time to chat about the mating bond a bit more seriously," Nereus says, breaking the silence.

Cleo agrees immediately, followed by me. We would both unquestionably mate with Nereus. Daisy hesitates.

"I want to," she says, "but what does it entail?"

Nereus explains the process to her. That it can be overtly sexual or that it can be a simple bite and promise to one another. That it doesn't have to be a huge claiming like maybe they've heard from their friends.

Daisy nods, "I like the sound of something more intimate like that. I wouldn't mind it ending up in sex, but I would want a clear head for it."

"We could do it this week, while we're here." Nereus suggests. My heart nearly bursts out of my chest with excitement.

"I would do it right now," Daisy says assuredly. "I love you." She tells Nereus. They share a kiss, and I hold Cleo close to me.

"I love you all," I say, earning kisses from my girls. We share a little moment together on my bench.

"Today it is, then." Nereus says, prowling towards us.

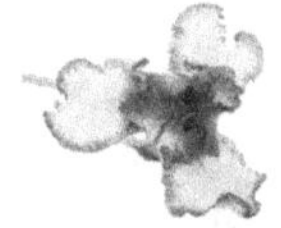

Nereus

I decided that we should do this in the spare bedroom, for a couple reasons. Mainly because I know we were about to make a mess. But also because this room is styled much closer to a typical nest, the bed sunken into the floor. Daisy and Cleo were initially fascinated by it.

We all strip our own clothes off, trying not to make the experience too sexual to begin with. Once we are all completely naked, our clothes in the corner, we all pile into the bed together.

Cleo sits in Daisy's arms, Daisy resting against Maddox, all facing me.

"Me, first." Daisy says, moving forward and claiming me in a kiss.

"I promise to love you, protect you, and care for you, Daisy." I say as we pull apart. I kiss down her neck, my tongue darting out and tasting the spot.

My teeth sink into her neck, lapping at the blood that pools there. She tastes of winter nights, black plums, dark cherries, cloves and all spice. It's delicious.

"Oh," Daisy moans in pleasure at my bite. I can feel our connection forming, our emotions entwining. I lick her wound closed before pulling her up to kiss me again.

It's a struggle to let her go to Cleo as Maddox makes his way to me.

"I love you," Maddox says as he kneels before me.

This is something I have wanted to happen for six years, I can hardly believe it's real.

"I am so happy we are finally coming together, my love." I say as I bite down on his neck. We both groan, deep and passionate sounds. The familiar scent of pine, amber and chestnuts is brought to life on my tongue.

Maddox barely lets me heal his wound before he pulls me into an almost aggressive kiss. I lose myself in it for a few minutes, but I eventually pull away to give my attention to my little princess.

Cleo comes to me and perches in my lap.

"You OK, princess?" I ask when I notice that her hands are shaking a little. She starts to cry at my question and my heart stops.

"I just love you all so much." She sniffles. "I love you so much, Nereus." I find myself tearing up at the look in her eyes.

I kiss her gently, moving towards her jawline and to her neck. I break her skin ever so delicately, the final bite connecting all four of us together. I carefully lap at Cleo's neck, her warm and sugary vanilla taste making my cock painfully hard.

Once she is healed, I kiss her again.

"I promise to protect you always, my love."

Chapter 52

C*leo*

A few weeks later

I toy with my hair, unsure of myself.

Everyone else had someone coming, except for me. I know I have Daisy's dad, but I'm not even sure how he's going to behave towards me.

"It's OK, princess." Nereus creeps up behind me, wrapping me in his arms and tentacles. "I promise you will have fun."

I try to relax back against him, but I'm too wound up. Our families were all meeting each other today.

Things have been great since our mating and coming back on tour. While we were gone, Nereus had commissioned some speedy alterations to the bus. And instead of bunks, we now had one really large bed to sleep in. It's not ideal for getting to the tub as we have to climb over it, but that's definitely easier than the makeshift bed we had.

It's also meant that we got some more upper cabinets for extra storage. Sebastian was getting a similar adjustment on their bus too, so I really think that's why we managed to get it done.

Tonight we were performing in our own city, in the new theater between the monster and human sides of town. It wasn't as big as any of the other venues we were playing on this tour, but it was important for us to play here.

Flora and Sebastian had known that they wanted to be the first people to perform here too.

That's where we are right now, in a reception room to have drinks with our families.

Nereus' mom and dad were the first to arrive, and they couldn't be any sweeter with Daisy and I. Maddox's mom and brothers make a straight beeline for Nereus, telling him it's about time. They're also pretty warm with us, his Mom asking us lots of questions.

When Daisy's dad arrives a little late, he skips right past Daisy and pulls me into his arms.

"You finally really are my daughter," he says.

I burst into tears, and Nereus is there holding me close and introducing himself. They instantly like each other, both just wanting to protect us girls.

I don't know why I was nervous at all. Everyone was so happy for us, and I felt so accepted.

Looking around at our families chatting, none of them really being *mine* before all this. I now know that I have such a big family, and such a wonderful home with my mates.

Epilogue

D*aisy*

Six months later

The warm glow of the sun on my skin is heaven.

Maddox and I are sunning ourselves next to the lake, while Nereus and Cleo are playing in the water.

We finished up tour a couple weeks ago, and since we had nothing on our schedules for a while… We decided to spend a whole month at the lake house.

Nereus and Maddox were able to get us a permanent home too. It's near Flora and Sebastian's, a new build just like theirs. But while they wanted to renovate, I loved the clean and fresh aesthetic, so I didn't want much done to it.

I giggle to myself, remembering when Cleo and I had brought the guys to our storage unit to move our things to the house. They had been fuming at how crappy our unit was, giving the guy at the desk a real hard time.

The lake house has been blissful, though.

Cleo was getting really good at swimming, Nereus and her being in the water every day together. She comes splashing out of the water now, flopping between Maddox and I on the blankets, getting us both wet.

If it wasn't so hot, I might be mad. But the cool water is actually a relief.

"Wanna practice later?" Cleo asks, gesturing to our dance studio.

One of the nicest things Nereus has done for us was convert an old storage shed into a dance studio. Fitted with the best of everything and hooked up to the air conditioning.

"Yeah, but let's have some lunch first. OK?"

I decide to cool off in the water first, though. I kiss Maddox before wading into the water to hip height.

"Hi there, sweetheart." Nereus says, coming out of the water like a predator in front of me. I know better, though.

My alpha picks me up, spinning me around. He kisses my mating mark, holding me close.

The Zodiac Society

If you enjoyed this book, try out some of my other stories... Month one is free on my Patreon.

Twelve signs. Twelve creatures. One challenge that could change everything.

When a freshman astronomy student stumbles into a nightclub that doesn't exist on any map, she's not looking for magic. She's looking for somewhere—anywhere—to disappear. But what she finds instead is a shimmering pocket of enchantment hidden on campus: the Zodiac Society.

By morning, she's waking up in Zodiac House with a choice—forget what she saw and go back to her ordinary life, or take the Zodiac Challenge: seduce twelve paranormals aligned with the signs of the zodiac, and earn her place in the Society. The rules are outrageous. The reward? Power, freedom, and a new name: Astraea.

Her first assignment? Aries.

Blaze is a faun with smoldering eyes, a sadistic streak, and a taste for control. His element is fire—and he knows exactly how to wield it. In a night of sharp pain and blistering pleasure, Astraea is stripped down, opened up, and set ablaze—inside and out. She's never submitted to anyone before. She never knew she could.

But this challenge is more than a string of pleasure-filled encounters. As Astraea dives into this world of monsters, magic, and illicit seduction, she begins to feel a pull toward something deeper—especially from the three Society members tasked with guiding her through the challenge: cool, clever Winslow; golden-hearted Ellis; and commanding, mysterious Miles.

And beneath it all, her body is changing. Her senses are sharpening. Something inside her is waking up.

Astraea might have entered the Zodiac Society by accident. But she's not leaving by choice.

ARIES is a high-heat, monster romance novella set in a secret society of pleasure, magic, and transformation. Each novella in The Zodiac Society series features a new zodiac-inspired creature, a spicy standalone seduction arc, and a slow-burning emotional journey that culminates in a shared HEA.

You will receive a new short story, exclusive artwork, and a page straight from Astraea's secret journal every month!

A Note from Sofia

Thank you so much for deciding to pick up my book!

I write across the paranormal and omegaverse romance genres, please check out my other books if that interests you.

To stay in the loop, scan the QR code for my important links, or go to https://sofiaroseauthor.com/

To be updated of even more news, consider signing up to my newsletter on my website.

Iris

A Monster MMFF Romance

A cinnamon roll minotaur. A stoic kraken. Two human omegas caught in the middle.

Daisy's job is simple: keep the choreography running smoothly and her best friend Cleo out of trouble. But when the tour heats up, so does the tension between them—and the band they're stuck sharing a bus with.

Cleo's always been carefree, but something about Daisy makes her want to be more. Especially when their flirty moments turn breathless... and the boys start paying attention.

Maddox is sweet, steady, and terrible at hiding how much he cares. Nereus is all hard lines, stormy eyes, and silent stares... but when the alpha drummer looks at them, he sees everything. Including the bond none of them were ready for.

Now four hearts are tangled together backstage, and holding back is no longer an option.

If you love cozy monster romance, submissive heroines, poly dynamics, and spicy omegaverse heat... you'll devour *Iris*.

F/F/M/M Poly Romance

Tentacles, Knotting & Heatplay

Found Family Tour Bus Chaos

Minotaur Sweetheart + Kraken Dom

Cinnamon Roll x Stoic Alpha tension

Fall hard with *Iris*, Book Three in the Fortune Records

Omegaverse series—standalone HEAs, monstrous spice, and a soft center every time.

www.ingramcontent.com/pod-product-compliance
Lightning Source LLC
Chambersburg PA
CBHW071556030726
47593CB00001BA/181